SAGITTARIUS

EDITED BY AUSTIN P. SHEEHAN
& HELENA MCAULEY

THE ZODIAC SERIES

The Zodiac Series is a collection of twelve speculative fiction anthologies, each focusing on one of the Zodiac signs. The anthologies feature short stories and poems inspired by each sign, and retellings of the various myths behind those signs.

#

Capricorn Aquarius Pisces

Aries Taurus Gemini

Cancer Leo Virgo

Libra Scorpio Sagittarius

#

The Zodiac Series has been produced by Australian Speculative Fiction, and each anthology contains a diverse selection of tales by talented writers from Australia and New Zealand.

First published by Deadset Press in 2021.
© Deadset Press 2021
All rights reserved.

Cover design Copyright © Austin P. Sheehan.
Edited by Austin P. Sheehan and Helena McAuley
Foreword by Sasha Hanton.

ISBN: 978-0-6450228-4-1

In the spirit of reconciliation, Deadset Press acknowledges the
Traditional Custodians of country throughout Australia and
their connections to land, sea and community. We pay our
respect to their Elders past and present and extend that respect
to all Aboriginal and Torres Strait Islander peoples today.

I AM SAGITTARIUS

Zoey Xolton

I am the Archer and my constellation is Sagittarius.
My tarot card is Temperance; I am an avid adventurer and
optimistic individual.
At my best I am generous, idealistic and humorous.
At my worst I am impatient, loud-mouthed and undiplomatic.
Energetic and wild, like my element: Fire, mine is a Mutable
sign.
I appreciate freedom, travel, philosophy and being outdoors.
However, I dislike clinginess, boredom and being constrained.
I am ruled by Jupiter, and am guardian to the fourth day of the
week.
My colours are blue and purple.

About the Author:

Zoey Xolton is an Australian Speculative Fiction writer, primarily of Dark Fantasy, Paranormal Romance, and Horror. Her works have appeared in over one-hundred themed anthologies, with more due for publication!

She has recently celebrated the release of her debut short story collection Darkly Ever After. *You can find further details regarding her many publications on her website: www.zoeyxolton.com!*

CONTENTS:

FOREWORD

Sasha Hanton

Adventurous, optimistic, and free-spirited are the terms often ascribed to Sagittarius natives. Represented by the centaur archer, the ninth sign of the zodiac—the mutable fire sign—is ruled over by planet Jupiter.

The constellation of Sagittarius has an interesting mythology behind it, with a debate as to which Greek figure of myth it represents. Known for portraying a centaur archer, the first figure often ascribed to the constellation is Chiron, an exception amongst the savage and brutal race of the centaurs. Whilst hunting alongside Heracles (Hercules)—or in one version simply keeping eye over a fight between Heracles and his fellow centaurs—Chiron was accidentally shot by Heracles with a poison arrow. As Chiron was immortal it did not kill him, but instead caused him immense suffering. Heracles, wanting to help Chiron, offered him the option to replace Prometheus. As punishment for giving humanity fire, Prometheus was chained to a giant stone and every day had his liver eaten by an eagle, only for it to grow back and the cycle to repeat. Chiron accepted the offer to replace Prometheus and was allowed to die. In commemoration, Zeus placed his image in the stars, or in some versions, let him take his final resting place in the heavens. There is some debate as to whether Chiron is the constellation Sagittarius or the constellation Centaurus, and some suggest that—considering Sagittarius is aiming an arrow at the heart of Scorpio—it could not be the gentle centaur Chiron.

Another Greek myth suggest that Sagittarius was a different centaur, a hunter who was placed into the heavens to ensure Scorpio didn't attack Orion again. However, there is another prominent Greek myth associated with Sagittarius that suggests the constellation is in honour of Crotus. The son of the god Pan and Eupheme (nursemaid to the muses), Crotus was a satyr who became an accomplished hunter and musician—in some tales he is the inventor of archery. As he had grown up with the muses, they begged Zeus award him with a constellation befitting of his great gifts.

Of course, the Greeks were not the only ones who had myths relating to the constellations. The Babylonians associated the constellation with Nergal, God of Pestilence, Plague, Death, and the Underworld. Nergal was depicted with two heads—one human and one panther—as well as a set of wings, and a scorpion's stinger positioned just above a horse's tail.

FOREWORD

Besides a rich mythology, Sagittarius—along with the other signs of the zodiac—shares ties to the Major Arcana of Tarot. The Temperance card in particular is linked to the archer constellation. Represented by a winged angel, with the sign of the sun on his forehead and the sign of the sacred book of the tarot on his chest, pouring what is meant to be the essence of life from chalice to chalice. In the process of slowly switching the liquid between each cup the angel is 'tempering' it. In fact, this is what the card is all about tempering and reaching an ideal middle; divinatory meanings for the card include modification, coordination, adaptation, and successful combinations. Sagittarius natives themselves are always seeking a perfect middle between the physical and philosophical, being a fire sign, they have a great passion for seeking out new places to travel and new ideas. The reversed meanings of the Temperance card also work as a warning against pursuing too many things at once, symbolising bad combinations and conflicts of competing interests.

Often called the ultimate free spirit of the zodiac, Sagittarians are ruled over by the planet Jupiter, named for the Roman counterpart of Zeus, the Greek ruler of the gods. Jupiter imbues those under its reign with good cheer, confidence, and a lightning bolt of energy. Those born between November 22nd and December 21st are crowned by a desire to explore, a competitive spirit and a passion to discover new

3

things—be it knowledge, places, or something spiritual. However, they can also be prone to restlessness.

Sagittarius is constantly on the hunt as it makes its way through the stars, just as those it influences are continually seeking out new adventures of one kind or another. With this anthology let yourself explore an endless list of possibilities and countless thrilling adventures, temper your mind's appetite with one story after another and embrace the hunt for finding out which is your favourite.

About the Author:

Sasha Hanton grew up living in the tropics of Darwin, Northern Territory (Larrakia Country). From a young age, she devoured books and iced coffee, both of which she continues to intake on an almost daily basis. Now living on beautiful Bribie Island in Queensland (Gubbi Gubbi Country) her time is split between writing and spoiling her dogs, Miley and Akela.

Sasha, who has a Bachelor of Journalism from Bond University, has dabbled in the journalistic profession but finds fiction far more fascinating. Coming from a multicultural background (Eurasian) she aspires to make her writing inclusive for people from all walks of life and to bring a unique blend of eastern and western culture to her writing. Throughout her life, she has been a lover of history and mythology, and frequently finds some way to worm one or the other into her storytelling. When she's not writing or reading she can be found walking her dogs and volunteering.

You can keep up with her writing at www.theshortstorypress.wordpress.com

TRACEY, DESTROYER OF WORLDS

Eva Leppard

Tracey clasped her hands behind her back, stretching absentmindedly as she looked out over the nothingness.

The absolute nihilism of unending nothingness.

Well, not absolute nothingness, she corrected herself. There was still *something.* A good sight less than there had been five minutes ago, a monochromatic expanse of rock and sand and some mountainous things in the distance. A blue sky fading to black indicated the existence for the time being of an atmosphere. But without anything for the atmosphere to coddle or cocoon it could afford to go too, she decided.

"Is that good enough?" she called out to the man behind her. She didn't bother to turn to face him; he knew who she was talking to.

"Well." A tremulous voice came through the ether to her headset. "What do you think? Do you think it's good enough? I mean, You're the expert."

She tapped her boot on the cracked dry ground, tiny eddies of dust puffing up from her toes. "You're right. We should send them back right to the beginning. New planet and all. This lot clearly couldn't be trusted. Let's see if they can manage a better job next time."

"So one more notch than 'Scorched Earth'?" came the voice again. "That would be . . . 'Ruination Beyond Belief'."

"No, look, I think we'll go 'Emptiness of a Mindless Void'. We haven't done that one in a while."

There was a silence, just long enough to indicate disapproval, but not long enough to approach disobedience.

"Are you sure?"

"Yeah, go on. Live a little. Hang on till I get back in though."

Within moments she had swung herself up onto the step of the slowly rotating glass orb that hung in the air, and ducked into the seat next to Pulsin. It was a snug fit, designed for rapid movement rather than cruising or style, and there was just room for her and the small creature manning the controls.

"Right," she said. "Do that thing that you do, bro-ski."

Another small pause.

"I do wish you wouldn't call me that."

"Oh get away with you. You love it. Go on, push the big red button. We've got places to be."

"I'd rather *you* press that one, if it's all the same to you." His voice had moved to an octave beyond tremulous, and now hovered somewhere around abject horror. "I really have quite a deep-seated ethical issue with—"

She slammed her hand down on the red button positioned on the ceiling above the driver's side door. Instantly the craft was jolted backwards, thrown as if on a rollercoaster ride that was serviced far less than recommended. Tracey felt her head crack against the headrest, and Pulsin gave out a little screechy groan. She grabbed the arm rest and grinned. This was the bit she liked. This was the bit that she was here for.

A manic, spinning feeling, darkness all around them for who knew how long then the gradual coming to rest, the spinning that slowed imperceptibly, until they were rotating gently, surveying what now finally could be described as:

Absolute nihilism of unending nothingness.

There it was.

Pinpricks of light in the distance all around them, but so far away as to challenge the concept of 'empty void' at all. The star that was the head of this local solar system shone at their backs, and Tracey was glad that she wouldn't have to be the one to break the news to it that it was now down one planet.

7

"Well that's that then," said Pulsin, his tone unnecessarily terse. "You can't get *that* one back, can you?"

The stars became streams of silver as the craft sped off.

"Do I detect a note of disapproval?" Tracey asked.

"Disapproval? Me?" Pulsin replied.

They sat for a few more moments, deep in what was a disapproving silence.

"It's just that you're supposed to use that as a last resort, not as a kind of way of clearing out planets that you don't like the coordinates of. It's meant to be used once in a . . . millennia even. Not a weekly occurrence. Someone is going to notice, you know." Pulsin's lips had narrowed.

"Oh rubbish, no one's going to notice. Everyone is quite busy enough dealing with their own areas, happy in the knowledge that I'm doing my job competently. And it's not like I leave anyone around to report back, do I?" She giggled.

"People are going to notice. People are going to notice that planets are going missing. They're going to check. Everyone isn't as stupid as you think they are."

"Bet you five-hundred rarks that they don't." Pulsin's comments were starting to annoy her now. "You know that this is my job, don't you? I'm not just a maverick careering around the galaxy willy-nilly destroying civilizations like some kind of a power-hungry warlord. There is a process, you know. I have to fill out check boxes."

Pulsin's lips had now narrowed so much they were invisible to the naked eye. "You have started taking diabolical liberties, and we both know it. You are supposed to *tweak* things to bring them back in line for the Greater Good. *Tweak*, I tell you. Cause the downfall of a leader here. Inexplicably wipe out a civilization there, yes. An *occasional* act of complete destruction. *For a very good reason.*"

Tracey crossed her arms and breathed out through her nose. She let her head press into the headrest. "There is always a good reason."

"Really? Would you just jog my memory about why that last planet is now a stream of atoms randomly careering around space?

For someone who was essentially just her driver, he was getting opinionated. She might have to do something about that.

"I don't want to share space with a planet that thinks that putting toilet paper on the roll back to front is a reasonable way to live, alright? That kind of thing should not be tolerated."

"Can you hear yourself right now?"

"I hated the way they had started building those condos too. The pink ones. That was an architectural disaster waiting to happen. And time-shares for crying out loud. Who still does that? A do over was the only option."

"Have you ever considered that this is more about you than them?"

9

To her left was absolute blackness. They must be on the very edge of the galaxy now. To the right there was the usual blazing glory of the middle of the galaxy, untold numbers of stars and nebulas and planets, all doing god knows what with their time.

She sighed. "Maybe you're right."

"They should never have given a control freak this job," Pulsin muttered, half to himself.

Keen to drown out his disapproval, she waved her hand in the air and conjured up a news report. Nothing local, of course, but galactic news was often a macrocosm of the micro . . . or something. Amongst quite a lot of static there was breaking news about the President of the Galaxy disappearing. *That will put the cat among the pigeons,* Tracey thought. The only thing holding the loose conglomeration of star systems, black hole neighbourhoods and cluster cul-de-sacs together was the president. Her ability to tread the fine line between listening ear and steely decision maker had averted many potential wars.

"She'll probably turn up eventually. Probably just needed a holiday." Summoning up the next job, Tracey flicked through the pages in the air in front of her. "Okay, so what we have here is a basic check-up . . ."

"You hear that? A check-up. That's all—"

"A basic check-up," she continued, raising her voice, "on a civilization that is, and I quote, 'teetering on the brink of a grave civil crisis'."

Pulsin glanced over to the words that hung in front of her. "What constitutes a 'grave civil crisis'? Non-specific phrasing like that gets you into trouble. And who is writing these things these days? We haven't been back to head office for so long; goodness knows who's in charge. Do you even know?"

She flicked through to the last page, looking for a signature. "No idea. But it's on the official letterhead." She peered at it, trying to decipher a name or a rank, or even a department. "Look, we just have to assume that the intel is good, alright?"

"A check-up," confirmed Pulsin.

"That's right."

He gave her a sidelong glance. "And you're ok with that?"

Tracey held her hands up in a gesture of surrender. "I am absolutely thrilled with a check-up. A check-up is literally the best thing that could be happening to me right now." She pressed the vapor-crypto lock that held the two of them in suspended animation for the duration of the interminable journey, reclined the seat as much as possible, and contemplated her life choices.

The galaxy passed them by.

Stepping out of the pod, the heat from the two suns was what first hit Tracey. Epsilon Sagittarii was how the system was known at home. Nuntuk, according to the locals. Either way, binary systems were always tricky. Not the least of their faults, in her opinion. The inhabitants had a certain edginess, a bleariness of thought and irrationality that made them difficult to deal with. The second thing to hit her was that the pod could not have settled itself in a less conspicuous place. They'd landed in the middle of a large plaza teeming with beings of all makes and models, all looking frightfully busy and important. She made a mental note to chastise Pulsin on his coordinate research skills. Not Landing In The Middle Of A Public Place was something even first year drivers had sussed.

Tracey glanced around. They *were* inconspicuous, apparently. Well, no one was paying any attention to them, anyway. Tracey and Pulsin, and the Orb they had emerged from, had been utterly unnoticed.

Well then. That was good.

Tracey pulled the spec sheet from the portal and checked the details. *'Find Uruchan. He'll be somewhere.'* Concise.

Once upon a time she'd been given spec sheets that spanned multiple pages, finishing with flow charts to track possible outcomes of potential actions. This new streamlined approach suited her much better. *More room for creative interpretation.*

And as long as her pay checks continued to be deposited into her Gradilarian account, she was happy to let sleeping dogs lie.

As if reading her thoughts, a bipedal creature scampered by her. Roughly dog-sized, furry and with a wagging tail, although its scales were where the canine resemblance ended.

"What's the plan?" Pulsin asked.

She strode off. Walking purposefully and in a way that indicated great strength of character was a neat little trick she'd picked up from a mercenary working on one of the mining moons off Jupiter. Stride purposefully and 99% of people will just be glad you're taking some sort of action and will let you get on with it.

"We're looking for Uruchan," she said to him over her shoulder.

"Who?'

She stopped, looked around. Busy area. Stone. Hot.

"Do you know where he is?" Pulsin was looking nervous again.

She shielded her eyes. She bloody hated binary systems. One day she'd like to be in the position to retire binary systems entirely. "Somewhere. He's somewhere."

"People are starting to look at us funny," he hissed back. "I think we've been noticed."

"Don't be ridiculous, there are fifty different species in this square alone. What possible interest would there be in—"

A large hand clamped down on Tracey's shoulder and lifted her off the ground, just a little. Enough to make it clear that being carried was an option. Just in case running was an idea that had flitted through her head.

She fixed her face into the 'bemused but open-hearted tourist' mode. She hadn't needed this one for a very long time, but it slipped back on easily, and Tracey turned with a slight smile.

She had to crane her neck to see the top of the body that the large hand was attached to. The top bit was blocking one of the suns, a fact that she considered thanking it for, but decided against it rapidly. It was not a face that needed thanking.

"Come with me." The face seemed not so much grown as hewn out of wood. Or stone. Something unforgiving and difficult to shape into a pleasing visage.

"Sure," she said as Pulsin ducked away and retreated back to the orb. *One less thing to worry about.* "Are you Uruchan?"

The hand was still clasping her shoulder and pushing her along, hurrying her. She didn't attempt to shrug it off; she would not, she knew, come out of any altercation as the winner. She quite liked her clavicles and wanted to keep them.

"Well I guess you'll let me know when you want my input then."

After some steering, she was veered off to the left and pushed through a hessian curtain. Standing in a small building made of mudbrick and straw, with a roof just high enough to take her full height, Tracey blinked into darkness. The contrast between the two suns and the gloom within threw her more than she'd like to admit.

The creature attached to the hand had not followed her inside. This, she imagined, was pure good manners rather than anything else, given that he would have brought the roof down if he had tried to shoehorn himself in. His shadowed bulk loomed just outside the curtain, his boots visible below it, facing away.

A shuffling sound drew her attention to a small creature, one of the bipedal dog things, as it emerged from a pile of hay. The creature jumped up onto a rough table and started at her. Its red beady eyes and pointed nose were fairly unnerving when attached to two legs and a human looking mouth. An unappealing creature all around. What had evolution on this planet been thinking?

Or maybe they used a different system.

"You took your time."

"I'm sorry?"

"I've been waiting for you."

"Uruchan?"

The animal gave a little bow. "At your service."

"Are you really?"

"Am I really what? Uruchan, or at your service."

She thought for a moment. "Both."

"Fair question. Yes, that is my name but no I'm not at your service."

"Good line though."

"I like it." There was a pause. "So yes, I've been waiting. I was under the impression that you were going to be here days ago."

She tilted her head to the side, wondering if this, also, was part of the schtick. "I'm wondering if you might think I'm someone else."

"You're Tracey, right."

"Oh ok. You do know who I am"'

"Tracey, Destroyer of Worlds."

"Sssshhhhh." She motioned him to be quiet with her hands, her eyes darting around to make sure no one had heard this. "Come on, keep it down. That's a strictly guarded code name."

"No it's not. Everyone knows about it."

"Everyone who?"

"Everyone who is anyone."

That didn't help much.

"I should clarify, anyone who is affiliated with the GlanMorian Cluster."

16

Hmmm. That made more sense. He knew about the GlanMorian Cluster. Her bosses. The shadowy cryptocracy that was in charge of most of the things that happened 'off the books' as it were.

"So you're part of the GlanMorian Cluster, are you?"

Uruchan raised one fuzzy eyebrow. "Involved, at least."

"What, here? In a barn?"

"Perfect cover."

"Well yes, alright, fair enough. But what am *I* doing here?"

"We want to discuss your career."

"My what?" Tracey frowned, wondering exactly how much they knew.

"They're not that happy with you, unfortunately."

She smiled in what she hoped was a broadly encompassing and reassuring manner. "I would like to explain to you just how confused I am, but I'm afraid that I'm too confused to do it."

"Would you care to sit down?"

She glanced around. "Where?"

"I don't know. It's what people say, isn't it? In these kinds of circumstances."

"Would you be able to clarify just what kind of circumstance this is?" She had a stirring of deep discomfort in her belly. The feeling that things might be about to become quite problematic.

"Your actions have not been going unnoticed," said Uruchan.

"Actions. Which actions in particular?"

"Not the standard stuff," he said, brushing away her words. "Not the normal stuff. That's all fine. We need someone mopping up mistakes around here after all, don't we? Tweaking the cosmic balance and all. It's just that, that last one . . ."

She thought back to the last one. "Yes."

"There was a Krillian on the planet."

Shit. She swallowed. "Well, that changes things."

"It does somewhat."

She decided that she did need a bit of a sit down and the nearest pile of straw would do perfectly well at this short notice.

Krillian. The most adorable and innocent creatures in the known universe. Utterly beloved by every civilisation, even the ones that sacrificed their own babies with their bare hands as a character-building exercise. Krillian, beloved and cherished younger sibling of every creature in the universe.

"However, I have a proposition for you."

"I didn't know," Tracey whispered, not hearing his words.

"Yes, yes, obviously. You wouldn't have done it otherwise, You're not a complete monster. But I'm afraid . . ."

"Yes?"

"You're not very popular at the moment."

"How could that have happened," she said, more to herself than anyone else. "Aren't they supposed to be guarded by

Shields of Mutual Adoration? I should have been notified when I entered the Atmos-space."

Uruchan regarded her wryly, his tail waving gracefully through the air as he spoke. "Would you have taken any notice?"

"Of course," she spat at him. "Of course I would have taken notice."

"So, my proposition?" he repeated. "Given that you are now, you know, universally derided and reviled amongst not only the populace but also the major governments?"

"The populace have never had a problem with me."

"No but they would if they had known about you."

He made a fair point.

Her head dropped into her hands. If word got out, then this really would change everything. She would have to find somewhere to hide out . . .

A sheaf of light flashed into the room as the curtain was pulled back, and another person ducked inside. A man, by the general size and shape, although he was fully clothed so it was hard to tell. The humanoid form was a pretty general prototype. His dark skin and black hair gave nothing away about his place of origin. His plain clothes were only embellished by a communications sheath above his wrist.

"This her?" he asked, raising his eyebrows at Tracey.

Uruchan nodded.

19

The man shook his head. "You are in trouble, lady. What were you thinking? Are you just a total sociopath or suicidally insane? Both?"

Tracey wished that she had a paper bag to hand. She focused on breathing in and out smoothly.

"I was just about to speak with her about her . . . options, shall we say. Tracey, meet Tragil. Tragil meet Tracey."

Tracey gave him a wan little wave; she was putting most of her energy into not fainting.

"I thought that her options involved never getting another job because she's now an utter pariah and no one would touch her with a ten-foot pole?" he said.

"Well yes, that is definitely something that has been bandied about, but there is something shall we say, more lucrative, that we have to offer the young lady."

Stabilising herself through sheer force of will she pointed at Uruchan. "That," she said. "That kind of thing. I'd like more talk of that sort of thing thanks. Not," and at this she waved towards Tragil, "Not that other sort of thing. I like what you're saying."

"Quite. Well, I thought that you might like to discuss an option that is somewhat out of the ordinary, but may serve to be an excellent solution to all concerned."

"Go. Do it. Let's hear it."

"You might have heard about the fact that the galaxy is currently, shall we say, without our dear and beloved leader."

"Oh yes I'd heard something. Vaguely. Somewhere. On holiday, was it? A constitutional of some sort?"

"Yes, that's the story that we have released. However, the leader is dead." Uruchan's large ears flattened slightly with this statement.

"Dead?"

"Dead. Again."

"Again? She makes a habit out of this does she?"

Uruchan glanced over at Tragil, who shrugged. "It was your idea."

"We've had, to be frank, a series of insipid leaders over the last five years none of whom had neither nous, tact, people skills, or ability to duck and weave when there's a flap."

"I'm sorry but I'm having a hard time understanding all of this."

"You said she was good," said Tragil, with a disappointed sigh.

"She is, she is. I have it on good authority that she is. Just bear with me."

He spoke a little more slowly. "You're aware of the leader of the galaxy, right?"

"Yes, she's fabulous. Everyone likes her. I voted for her."

"And she's never killed a Krillian," said Tragil as an aside.

21

"Well I should inform you that she died shortly after her galactic election win, five years ago."

"That was careless of her."

"It was quite a disaster," continued Uruchan, ignoring her. "All that democratic process up the gurgler. We certainly weren't going to go to all that bother again. But yes, as I said, she had an unfortunate accident with a corkscrew, a saucepan lid and a pot plant a few weeks into her stint and so, ever since then, we've been . . . covering it up."

"Covering it up? Covering up the fact that the President of the Galaxy has been dead for five years? How the hell do you cover something like that up?" Tracey was sounding more and more interested in the conversation

"You literally destroy planets and no one has twigged to it yet. Do you really think we can't cover up a dead leader or two?" offered Tragil.

Tracey held up her hands. "All right, assuming that I believe you, what has this got to do with me? Also who is 'we'?"

"We are a concerned group of active citizens closely aligned with the GlanMorian Cluster who are interested in getting the galaxy back on a steady footing."

"Back? When was it ever on a steady footing?"

Noises came from outside the room, and more booted feet had joined the boots of Weighted Meaty Hand.

Uruchan threw Tragil a look, and Tragil ducked out of the room. "To put it simply, we have been using stand-ins as the galactic president since then; some basic facial terra forming and voice modulations have managed to fool most people, but unfortunately the stand-ins just haven't been up to the job. We have had trouble finding people with the general quick thinking and open-minded, concise decision-making, coupled with the people skills and sheer bloody-mindedness needed to get the job done. They keep getting assassinated, you see."

"They *keep* getting assassinated. Surely that's more the fault of the security detail than the poor stand-in?"

"Could be, could be," mused Uruchan.

Tragil stepped back into the room. "No problem," he reported. "Just someone needing some hay."

"We'll be out of here in a minute."

"Yes, that's what I said."

"As I was saying, they have all been spectacularly unsuited for the job, which is where you come in, of course. We have been following your . . . progress, and we think that you would be extremely well suited to it. So we'd like to offer it to you."

"Offer me the what?"

"The job. Leader of the galaxy."

Tracey glanced around. "A dog, in a barn that's being hired by the hour, is asking me if I want to be the leader of the galaxy."

"Essentially yes. This is what we have been reduced to, but it might serve to remind you that your options are now limited. Your job as . . . whatever you want to call it has of course been terminated due to an unfortunate event with a Krillian, all of your official recompenses and gratuities have been revoked, your work-vehicle has been dispatched home, so if you don't say yes, then you're essentially on this god-forsaken planet that no one's ever heard of for the rest of what may well be a spectacularly unpleasant yet probably brief, life."

Tracey though for a moment. "I'd prefer not to be assassinated."

"Oh go on." Uruchan laughed, a curious barking sound. "You've been judged to be pretty much assassination proof. Even taking into account what you point out is inept security measures. No, your past, personality and capabilities have all been carefully assessed and, out of everyone in the galaxy—at least the bits that matter—you are, as they say, It. You're it. You're the absolute best we can do."

"You sound thrilled."

He spread his hands expansively. "It is what it is."

"Is there anything in it for me?"

"Apart from being the most powerful person in the galaxy?" She shrugged.

"Well, we will ensure that the small matter that you're a Krillian killer will be conveniently forgotten. You get to start again. Make decisions. Be someone."

She chewed on her lip. Maybe he was right. Maybe it was her only option. "Can I think about it?"

Tragil choked back a laugh as stone crunched under the wooden wheels of a wagon. "It's time," he said. "This is it. If you say no, then you'll head off for whatever awaits you. If yes, then—" he gestured to the metal contraption wrapped around his wrist "—we will open coms and have you up and running as the ruler of the galaxy within an hour."

"Come on," urged Tragil. "We need to get moving."

"All right," said Tracey after a moment. "All right, I'll do it on one condition. Is there the possibility for advancement?"

"Advancement from being the president of the galaxy? You want something up from that."

"You said that there's people behind the scenes, pulling strings, yeah?"

"Uruchan," Tragil's voice was now strained "We have to do this now. We'll miss the transport if we wait any longer."

"Pulling the strings," she repeated. "If I can do this without getting assassinated that would be the sensible next step. To be part of this 'bigger thing' you're talking about."

"All right," Uruchan snapped. "All right, if you can do this without getting assassinated then we can discuss some upward mobility."

Tracey held out her hand and Uruchan pressed his paw against it, the galactic symbol of honour.

"I don't quite know how we ended up here," muttered Uruchan, "but I suppose we're both getting what we wanted."

Tragil pressed his comms sleeve and the walls shimmered as connection was made with the transport ship circling in the thin atmosphere above.

"I guarantee it," said Tracey, as she grinned widely and the three bodies disintegrated as they were transported to the ship. "I guarantee that we will both get what we want out of this agreement. Now tell me, do I have any jurisdiction over binary systems at all?"

About the Author:

Eva Leppard lives in lutruwita (Tasmania) with an elegantly sufficient amount of children and a disturbingly large number of rescue animals, many of which she raised by hand whether they liked it or not.

She can be found wasting time on Twitter as @paranormaljunk2 or on FB at https://www.facebook.com/evaleppardauthor

Waste Not

Cassandra Hounsell

The Hunter found the droid with its skull cracked open, brains of copper line and rusted coils spilled down its neck, its memories picked clean. At its feet, once-human prey with twisted neck, flies slipping in and out of blue lips. The droid had been clutching the bow, a token taken from its prey. Knew it a weapon but not how to use it, had lifted it high like a club to swing. The Hunter had chuckled with their palms aloft.

I'll show you how to hunt, they had told the droid, *if you share with me your kill.*

With the Hunter, the droid learnt how to use the bow. The first few times the arrow hit askew and off balance. The next few took shards of skin and tasted blood. Soon enough, the Hunter was making good meals of fallen prey, for the droid had no use for its kills. The prey died screaming, an arrow protruding from the eye, hit through an open window.

The Hunter shared all but the meat with the droid; that they kept for themselves. Supple, hairless leather became ammo pouches slung across chest, around waist. Pale bone was used for knives, and hooks to catch the two-headed fish in the radiated river. The blood to use as paint.

Waste nothing, the Hunter had told the droid as they strung a wreath of teeth and gifted it upon the droid's crown. *Take all that you can use and leave only the trash behind. That's the way of this world.*

The red lights of the signs overhead, flickering as a fly spasms in its dying peril, dance over the metallic city. Blues and bottle greens that run golden where they meet in the laneways, at crossroads, tarnished silver at their edges where the poorest live. There the fences are built high to keep the wasteland beyond out, with its broken body creatures and radiation clogged rivers and drifters with gangrenous toes and milky-white stares.

The droid hates those fences. It had been one of those broken body creatures once, discarded and left to rot in the wastelands with the rest of the trash. It had fallen from the skies, the Hunter had told it once, tin angel shot down from the mountain of the gods by the one who ruled the skies, landing upon the garbage peak beneath the constellation of the Archer. Whether that was true or not—the droid did not

remember anything beyond waking up among trash—it liked
the story, appreciated the poetry of it. Although the Hunter
had not named the droid for those stars. Rather, the Hunter
had chosen the name because of the bow they had found it
with. The one that clacks upon its back, wood against metal,
chafing with every clanking step and hiss of piston as it hunts.

The droid's firelight optics cast glow over its angled cheeks
and onto the pavement underfoot, staving off the leeching
shadows sliding out of alleys and unlit doorways.
This city is a beautiful monster; it eats you up, digests what it
wants of you and filters out the rest, a shit heap of decaying,
damned, those all used up and dry.

Waste, such waste. It sickens the droid; the Hunter would
have hated this. Perhaps it is good they lived not long enough
to witness the rise of the city, built upon the festering soils of
the wasteland, erected from the bones and the blood of those
long left behind. They had forgotten that, the glittering people
with their lapis tongues safe inside their glass walls; their city
had risen by making use of all, of letting no death be in vain,
and they spat upon that memory.

The droid thumbed over the chamber of a gun, slung at their
hip from a strap woven of hair. They had found it where the
wastelands met the city, at the silver edges, at the fence. Took it
from the grey tips of a guard's outstretched hand. Found a knife
there too. Took that, took the coins, golden in the acid-wash sun.

Took the name tag and the badge that the guard had no more use for; it would have been wasteful to leave it.

The droid passes the people—insects rather—buzzing at the steps, leaning out the windows to breathe deep in the recycled air as the music thumps from the peeling buildings. Dark within and lit on the out with the signs in fluorescents, visages of alluring silhouettes, with promises of eager consorts with as many arms as it takes to please.

The insects open their lips to let the smoke collect at their brows, haloes of pollution hanging over these bacterial angels made from their own filth and sin.

The droid snorts; what pitiful creatures they are. What good ever came from a rabbit's warren of brain matter protected only by a thin veil of easily crushed bone? Or a set of lungs to draw in the sullied air, poison that cannot be escaped, that collects inside. What good had ever come from having a beating heart? They squander such gifts, contaminate them, let them go bad. They waste them.

Their Hunter was the only one who did not, the only one not insect but entirely person. But what good it had done them, anyway? They had died like every other fly, caught in a web.

The droid hunts the restless streets in the deepest hour of night, where the darkness fights its way to stay, sinks in its claws to leave its lasting memories before the light comes and makes them all forget. The day gives these insects a foolish notion of safety; that if they can see it, it poses little threat.

They don't seem to understand that the light offers them nothing that the dark does not. Neither are capable of stopping a bullet, the slender line of a knife across the throat, or an arrow through the eye. Neither stops the stench of rot that is bleeding in at the edges of the city, tarnishing the silvers and golds, pollution that cannot be kept at bay by a fence.

The droid passes through the red bloom tumbling out from the doorway and across the street. The lady insects leaning there cast ghoulish shadows, their legs long, tentacles coiled, nails and horns honed sharp at their tips.
The glow from the neon signs overhead stretches fingers, reaching for the wall of brick that stands across the walkway, the breast of the apartment block opposite scarred with paint and grime. There, where the crimson light is at its weakest, stand two more insects, their voices slurred and murky, grating to the droid's receptors.

One of them has his back to the world, facing the wall. His knees are spaced apart and his hands hidden from view, and the toxic liquids he ingested earlier now pour out from between his legs, splashing at his feet, a dark, jagged stain cast against the grey brick of the wall.

Beside him the other sways, bottle to lips. The liquid dribbles down his jaw, his feeble, meaty mind muddled and clumsy. At his feet are the remains of cigarettes, some burning still. The droid turns its face from them, narrows its optics to the ground. Disgusting, filthy. Rotting and wasteful. What trash they leave upon the planet, choke it with. One day what they throw into the gutter will rise again and swallow them all.

The bow clacks at the droid's back, the gun hanging from its waist, the knife glinting at its hip.

It steps out from the light of the doorway, moving onward back into shadow when a shout comes from behind. It denies them, continues on, and then the blow comes. The impact from the bottle rocks its head forward, the shards raining down over its shoulders, trickling like glittering sand onto the ground.

Waste, such waste.

It turns towards them, the grit of glass uncomfortable in its joints, and the insects jeer. The one with the bottle, now empty-handed and struggling to stand upright, has to catch himself with the wall behind him. The pisser with spattered boots sways on the spot. Finished, but his pants still gape wide. Their mouths are twisted, teeth both bone and jewel shining between peeling lips, the sound of them uneven and out of tune as it bounces around the alley. From the doorway, the ladies laugh.

Come here! One of the insects says, the one that had the bottle. *Come over here!*

What follows is a string of slurs, both in the way their numbed tongues can't quite form the words and in the degrading sense.

The droid watches them, then obeys.

The insects rejoice in their small victory, until they see the flash of steel as the droid pulls it from its hip.

Their hands are in front of them, soft palms raised in a pitiful effort of defence, and the knife is in the throat of the one that had once held the bottle. It is buried up to its hilt in the underside of his chin, his life spilling down his chest. He gives up trying to remain standing and drops first to his knees, then to his side.

The pisser's mouth hangs open like the insect he is, eyes bulging wide and white as he stutters back a step. The droid has him in a second, bone, sinews no match for the titanium that piece it together, and with a rotation, he too falls, head pulled at an angle not meant to be.

There is a scream, shrill and high and it slices, sharp, through the still night. Those lady insects aren't laughing anymore.

The droid turns from the bodies, from the blood mucking at its feet, goes to disappear back into the shadows where light has yet to touch when it pauses.

It looks back at the wall with the garish graffiti, arrogance scrawled in jauntily inked names and it looks at the bodies, insects still kicking, spasming in their dying peril.

Waste, such waste.

The droid kneels, picks over them in the way that a hunter searches for the good meat, the stuff in the rump, in the chest, finds a flask, a carton of unused cigarettes, a switch-knife carved with initials, a pocketful of assorted wrappers that crinkle to the touch. A jacket, leather worn and supple. They have no use for it, not any of that, nor their teeth that can be used for buttons. Their hair that can be woven into rope. Their guts that can re-string the bow. Their ribs that can make needles for etching, knitting, threading. The droid takes it all, leaves only the bits it has no use for but someone else may, leaves only the trash.

By the time the sirens come blaring the droid has already gone, stolen away with the retreating gloom, one of those shadows that seeps. When the light comes, they won't have forgotten this time; this city will not forget. There is no more discarding, no more leaving to rot in the wastelands. The filth, the trash tossed into the gutters has risen to swallow them up.

The droid pats the skull made into shoulder pauldron, traces their Hunter's sandblasted grin and thinks the smile is one of pride; they live on in a lesson, they died not in vain, their life made use of.

Nothing wasted.

About the Author:

Cassandra spends her days in the made-up worlds of her mind, with the people that live there. When she ventures into the land of the living, she runs creative writing groups for adults, teens and children.

CASSANDRA HOUNSELL

THE TALBOTVILLE CENTAUR

Tim Borella

The pass office was to the right of the gaol's main entrance,
where a large gate between two imposing bluestone turrets was
open to admit a laden dray pulled by a pair of fine Clydesdales.
The guard I followed was unimpressed at having been ordered
to escort me, no doubt in his view just another time-wasting
newshound. Down echoing corridors we walked, through
barred gates, across the forbidding square and past the
gallows—used less often nowadays but still quite ready to
perform its function—and through a door in a high wall, into a
compound within a compound. At last we reached the ugly
stone building that housed the object of my interest.

My reluctant guide used every key on the large ring clipped
to his belt to negotiate the series of locked doors leading into the
gloomy interior, where the silence was cut only by our footsteps
as we walked along a row of cells, all empty bar the last.

My first encounter with the prisoner was something of a disappointment. I had imagined a fearsome creature, and indeed he must have been at some time, to have ended up in this place reserved for the notorious and dangerous. But the figure I beheld was unimposing, slight even; an impression magnified by the outsized prison clothing he wore. His dark hair, long and wild at the time of his capture, had been hacked short, with strands of grey curving through it. He could have passed for one of the prematurely aged wastrels one often passed in Melbourne's dark laneways, and there was a corresponding stink in the cell to boot.

He had been brought in, still clad in the roughly cut hide of a stolen beast, following an extensive manhunt sparked by numerous complaints of unlawful interference with cattle, culminating in the death of a stockman who had attempted to thwart his actions. Months had now passed since his capture, and after an initial burst of excitement, the hubbub had just as quickly died down. The city was ever ready for some new sensation—the rumour of a new gold seam, murmurs of another royal scandal—so it was no surprise that the fickle focus of public attention had moved on. It would swing back if he were to hang, though, and I planned to be ready for that eventuality.

He sat huddled on the floor in the corner of the cell, even though both a hard bed and low bench were available. He did not raise his eyes when we entered, but he flinched as the key turned in the lock and I could tell he was watching me while pretending not to, a skill I myself was well practiced at.

Whether it was because the prisoner didn't appear capable of harming me, or that the gaoler didn't care if he did, he stepped back out of the cell and locked the door behind him.

"Shout out when you're finished," he ordered, already making for the guard's niche we'd passed on the way in.

I turned back to the man on the floor, who had shifted so he was now more side-on to me, his cheek pressed up against the hard bluestone. I stayed where I was, maintaining as much distance between us as possible in that small space. He was quiet but tense, his small sidelong glances and the rapid rise and fall of his chest giving him away.

"I won't hurt you, old fellow," I said, and felt immediately foolish. This was an accused thief and murderer, one who'd had the whole town talking, and yet in that moment not threatening but terrified. Perhaps it was just my imagination, but my impression was of an animal at bay.

I was fascinated by him, and found myself studying him as if he were an exhibit in a natural history museum. His feet were bare despite the cold, soles calloused and scored, and every inch of exposed skin bore some scar or blemish. The prison garb hid his proportions but there was a sense of wiry strength to him. A growth of coarse beard covered his jaw.

39

Without realising it, I'd crept closer until—with the speed of a striking snake—he jumped to his feet. I stumbled back, shocked, hands raised both in apology and in readiness for whatever he might try.

He was facing me, feet apart, dark eyes wide, nostrils flaring. For some seconds I was transfixed by his stare. It felt like an electrical signal passed between us, as if something beyond my ken was being communicated to me, and without rational basis, I understood my own eyes were sending a return signal, a message that I had not come to jeer or harm, but rather learn and understand.

Very slowly I retreated, until my back touched the iron bars. With that, he resumed his despondent huddle in the corner.

Approaching the guard's niche on the way out, I asked if I might trouble him with a question or two. At first he was cagey, but a couple of shillings and an assurance that any comments he made would be off the record saw a marked change in his demeanour. I started by asking him about the prisoner's routine.

"Well, he don't do much at all," he said. "Paced around a lot when he first came in, tried to rush out the door whenever he thought he had half a chance, but a touch of the lash soon settled that down. Wouldn't eat, neither—went about a week on just a few drops o' water. Oh—there's a strange thing as well! The beggar didn't even know how to use a cup, tried to suck the water out of the top rather than pick it up. He learned, though, I'll give him that. He ain't stupid, but . . . don't know how to put it, exactly. Doesn't seem to know anything much about anything. Can't talk, or won't, anyway. Even messed himself a couple of times, until we got him trained to use the bucket."

"I see," I said. "And how did you do that?"

A cruel smile creased the guard's stubbled face. "He don't seem to understand English, but—" he glanced at the short whip hanging on the wall, "—that there tends to break down language barriers without too much trouble."

Bishop set his tankard down and leant towards me across the dark wooden table of one of the Union Hotel's quieter booths. "I must tell you, Hawley, I think the whole story's a lot of rot."

"Maybe so," I said, "but you'd have heard the hysteria around town when they brought him in. Even if there's not a grain of truth in any of it, I'll bet I can put something together that will sell."

"Well, you've never let an absence of facts hold you back before, have you, old man?" he laughed. "Why start now, eh?"

"Why, I find that rather offensive!" I said, adopting an aggrieved look but unable to suppress a smile. My bookmaker friend and I went back a long way.

"You know, though," I continued, "there's something about this fellow that has me convinced he's more than just a common ruffian. I can't explain it, but now I've visited him a few times, I'm sure there's . . . I don't know, a kind of wild sincerity to him."

"Come on now," said Bishop. "The man can't even speak, can he? How can you comment on his character?"

I frowned. How indeed? And yet I was sure the odd communication between me and the prisoner was more than just a figment of my imagination. Still, putting that into words wasn't possible in the smoky ordinariness of our favourite watering hole. I tapped the dottle out of my pipe and reached into my waistcoat pocket for my tin, extracted an aromatic pinch, tamped it down and relit. My thoughts were as intangible as the rising smoke. "Yes, yes, you're right, I'm sure," I said. "Still, the whole improbable thing fascinates me for some reason. I just wish there was some way I could flesh the story out a bit. It seems to be all rumour and innuendo—my friend's cousin's father-in-law overheard someone say he thought he saw him, that kind of thing."

Bishop nodded and raised his hand to order us another round. "I tell you what, this may be an example of the very thing you're talking about, but I do happen to know a fellow." He paused, making me wait.

"And?" I said, intrigued but cautious not to take the bait too quickly. My friend didn't mind having a lend of a person now and then, though always good-naturedly.

42

"An old fellow, a cripple. A bit too fond of the drink, perhaps, but one can understand that. Hurt himself in a riding accident some years ago up in the mountains; in quite a bit of pain most of the time I gather, can't walk properly."

"Yes, yes," I urged. "Do get to the point."

"Well. I often see him poking about the racetrack. Not able to do much on account of the injuries, y'see, but the trainers all listen to him. Knows what he's talking about, one of those old bushmen who could ride before they could walk."

"And what does this have to do with—"

"Patience, old man. I'm coming to that." He took a sip of his beer and scraped the foam from his moustache with a quick movement of his bottom lip. "So," he continued, "this fellow— Dixon? Dutton? Something like that. Anyway, word is that when they brought your man in, the old boy was just about apoplectic. Went around telling all and sundry that this wasn't a man at all but a daemon, a half-man half-horse who'd been creating havoc up in the high country for years, wrecking fences and stampeding cattle over cliffs, running wild with the brumbies. Reckoned he'd seen him with his own eyes."

I raised an eyebrow. "Sounds like he does like a drink."

"Well, maybe so," said Bishop, "but I overheard him talking with a strapper about it, and while I grant you it sounded like a load of superstitious old poppycock, the impression I got was

43

that he wasn't just spinning a yarn. He sounded serious, and as you know, I'm a fair judge of these things."

Indeed he was. Bishop was a good companion and a jocular fellow, but also a shrewd businessman. I'd not yet met the person who could fool him.

"So even if what he said was impossible," I said, "he himself believed it?"

"Precisely."

"Well, that's a good start, at least. I get the impression that the real facts of this matter will remain a mystery, but when this wild man goes to the gallows—as I suspect he will—there's going to be a resurgence of public interest, and I intend to be ready for it. Will you put me in touch with this . . . what's his name?"

"Dalton! That's it." Bishop stroked his moustache, then gave a quick nod. "Yes, if you like."

A few days later I sat on a crowded tram, rocking gently as the sturdy horses in front pulled us along the tracks. With my brown leather briefcase resting at my feet, I was squeezed in between an older woman with a pile of empty hessian shopping bags and a young man in patched working clothes—a builder's labourer or bricklayer, judging by his sturdy build and calloused hands. I always enjoyed riding the trams, as they allowed me to observe my fellow Melburnians in all their variations whilst going about my daily business.

This day was overcast, with the odd sprinkling of rain as we travelled the Flemington line, being overtaken by sulkies and carriages, halting regularly at the various stops. Tall poplars lined the wide road, and a steady breeze ruffled their leaves while providing welcome relief from the infernal flies that were an unavoidable by-product of the copious piles of manure scattered about the streets by our equine-powered transport systems. Steam carriages—unreliable things based on the principle the trains used for locomotion—had been seen wheezing and popping around town in recent years, scaring horses and breaking down at inopportune times, and there had been reports of vehicles powered by the new internal combustion engines becoming popular overseas. Social grandstanding being what it was, I suspected it wouldn't be too long before they'd make their way to us and perhaps usher in a cleaner, more pleasant future.

For now, though, it was horses I was focused on, particularly their relationship to the prisoner. I didn't know what to believe of the florid rumours I'd heard about him, but there must have been at least some basis in fact for the troopers to have brought him in. He had been charged with murder and other serious offences under the Crimes Act, including cattle stealing, and numerous other matters ranging from petty misdemeanours such as the working of animals without consent of the owner, to the abominable crime of buggery with an animal. I was somewhat perplexed as to what evidence the prosecution might use to bring about a conviction on that last matter.

The conductor's shout brought me out of my reverie and I stepped down from the tram, pausing first to check the road was clear. A pregnant woman had been knocked down and her legs broken not a week before by a reckless young driver laying on the whip, more interested in the girl beside him than the road in front. I had not heard what had become of the unborn child, but could only assume that nothing good could come of such a shock.

On foot, I made my way down several side streets leading towards the racetrack, nestled into a wide bend of the Maribyrnong. The houses got shabbier as I walked, until I came to the address Bishop had given me. The dwelling was modest but clean, of weatherboard and corrugated iron patched with various boards and sheeting that did not match the original. I hesitated for a moment, then knocked at the door. I was about to knock again when I heard stirrings from inside, and a stout woman with her hair in a bun peeked around the edge of the door. I introduced myself, and satisfied that I was not a threat of any kind, the lady of the house advised that I should go around to the back of the premises, where I would find 'Old Thomas'.

I thanked her and picked my way through the overgrown citrus trees crowded between the side of the house and the wooden fence separating it from its virtual twin next door. A scruffy piebald dog poked its head around the edge of the building in much the same way as the woman had done at the door, then retreated, granting me entry to the small back yard. In the far corner was a rough shed which wouldn't have been out of place in a farmer's paddock, walled in on three sides, the fourth sporting a thick curtain made from wheat bags held aside by being thrown over the structure's top corner. Smoke rose from a small fire in a circle of stones just outside the entrance, and beside it on a low wooden stool sat a white-haired man, hunched over with elbows resting on knees, gazing at the glowing coals.

I cleared my throat and he looked up, blinking owlishly a couple of times.

"Good morning, sir," I said, as if the man was a banker and I had come to his office to apply for a loan. "I hope you don't mind the intrusion. I'm Theodore Hawley, and my good friend Mr Bishop suggested I seek you out as someone who is knowledgeable on the subject of horses."

He sat up, a pained expression crossing his face as he moved, but I could tell he was pleased to have been described thus. "I do know a thing or two about horses, that's true enough," he said, the hint of an Irish accent colouring his

47

words. "But what might you be wanting to find out about them from me, I wonder?"

Various items lay about in the hut, including an iron-framed cot and some pots and pans, and another stool.

"May I sit down?" I asked. "I'm a writer, interested in the experiences of cattlemen such as yourself in the high country. I do have a number of questions I'd like to ask, and I thought—if you don't mind, of course—we might talk for a while. Over a drink, perhaps?" I patted my briefcase, and the old fellow's demeanour brightened.

"Pull up a chair."

For the first half hour we spoke in general terms about his experiences as a younger man working cattle up in the hills and high plains stretching northward from Gippsland up into the alpine regions past Dargo and across to the Snowy River, where the weather could range from oppressive heat to bitter blizzard and a man needed his wits about him to survive, let alone keep vast herds of stock alive and safe.

I sipped from my tin mug of rum, while Tom, as he'd invited me to call him, took a more robust approach.

"Helps ease the joints a little," he said, setting his pannikin down on the ground beside him and gingerly shifting his posture.

As we talked, his observations moved from the factual—how he, the son of an immigrant labourer, had gained hard experience and come to be considered an expert in cattle handling in the alpine country—to more personal matters, like the effects of long spells alone with only cattle and horses for companionship; the certain knowledge that a serious accident or a snake bite would mean the end; the strange effects some places had on the mind so that stories of spirits and monsters that would seem laughable under normal circumstances became magnified to the point where men on their own could be driven mad by them.

He spoke of encounters with natives, common in his early experiences but rarer as men like he himself put up fences and denied them access to hunting grounds and waterholes in the quest to secure good pastures, or drove them like animals with whips and guns so there could be no question about who the ancient mountains and abundant high plains belonged to.

"And the horses!" said Tom, taking a good swig from his mug and looking away as if seeing a vision of his younger self galloping across a wide river valley in pursuit of errant strays. "Great mobs of brumbies, breeding up in the good seasons and hidin' God knows where in the winters. They could be a menace, cuttin' up the ground and fouling the waterholes, eating feed the cattle should have had, but by the Lord Harry, could the beggars run!"

The old fellow had been drinking freely but was not yet affected to the point where his perceptions were dulled and confused, and the time was now right to raise the subject I'd come to discuss.

"Tom," I said, "do you think there's any truth to the stories that have been going around about this fellow who's been brought in, the one they captured up near Talbotville?"

He quickly turned to me, his air of nostalgic reflection gone. "Oh, there's truth, all right," he said, eyes alive with intensity. I was afraid he might close up, but my instincts told me to continue questioning.

"Could you tell me a little of what you know?"

He was quiet for a time, staring back into the fire; then, he began to speak. "Most city folk don't know what it's like to live in the real world. They think what they see is all there is, but they are blind. I'm not talking about the kinds o' things my old mother—God rest her—used to go on about, spilling salt or never picking a white flower, but real things, things you see when you're properly on your own."

"And this man?" I said. "What about him?"

Tom ran his fingers over the grey stubble on his chin. "What about him? Well, Mister Hawley, I'll tell you this. I may be old and broken and a drunkard, but I am not mad, though plenty of people will tell you otherwise. The man you speak of, if he really is a man, is in league with the horses. He knows them, he speaks to them, he is one of them."

"And you have seen him?"

Again he was quiet, gathering his thoughts before continuing. "I'd heard talk for years, which I took as bungler's excuses for lost cattle, or else made-up fancies, like stories about bunyips and ghosts. Then, spring of seventy-three, when the weather was warming up and I was bringing a mob up along the Crooked River, I camped for a spell on a nice wide bend with plenty of feed. Nights were quiet, but after I'd been there a few days the cattle started getting stirred up for no reason. I'd get out of my swag and scout around, but apart from the odd wild dog, I wouldn't find anything.

"Then, this night, I woke to a mad rush. The cattle were everywhere, and for a minute I thought I might be trampled where I lay. Well, I jumped up and ran for my gelding, who I'd hobbled and staked, but when I got to him, he'd broken the tether and was lurching around fit to bust himself. The air was thick with the sound of pounding hooves, galloping horses, and in the moonlight a great mob of them circled around us like the devil himself was chasing them.

"I managed to get the bridle on my horse and throw the saddle over him and got on with no idea of what I might do, but I had to do something, otherwise the cattle would be spread from there to New South Wales. I rode out towards the front of that mob of brumbies with my stockwhip ready thinking I might be able to drive them off, but as I came at them, they turned away by themselves and raced off towards the hills."

"What did you do then?" I asked, caught up in his tale.

"Well, I thought I was all right, because they were gone and I'd be able to round up my cattle and go back to sleep, but when I tried to turn my horse there was no stopping him. I've ridden some hard-mouthed scrubbers in my time but Samson himself couldn't have dragged the reins hard enough to pull this fella up, and he was normally gentle as a lamb.

"We were racing along flat out and I thought about jumpin' off before he put his hoof in a wombat hole or smashed me into a tree branch, but I ain't never been one to bail, and half of me wanted to see what this mob of horses was up to, besides. The moonlight was bright enough to see, so I just hung on, and we kept going. After a while we caught up with the mob, and my horse ran alongside them like a fish in a school. Nothing I could do would turn him or slow him down, and I could have jumped on to the backs of the brumbies beside us, they were so close. The sound of their hooves—it was like thunder! Then, as we came alongside a rise, something made me look up."

I leaned forward, caught up in the mad ride with him.

"And there, up on the hillside, was another group of horses, and as we passed they came galloping down to join the race. And on the back of one, or maybe part of one, or so it looked to me, with his body cloaked in fur, his bare arms ready to strike, and his hair flowing out behind him like a mane, was this man, or beast. He flew down towards me like an angel, shouting in some language nobody'd ever heard, and as he did so the horses beside us turned at his command and pushed us off our course. I looked ahead and I saw we were coming to the edge of a scarp, and yet those horses kept pushing us towards it."

"What happened then?" I said, breathless.

"We went right over the edge, my old horse and me," he said, eyes locked with mine.

I raised my mug and took a good mouthful, hardly noticing the burn.

When we had both recovered our equilibrium somewhat, I was able to tease out the rest of Tom's story. By some miracle, he had survived the fall, though grievously injured. He didn't remember much of the aftermath, but thought his horse must have taken most of the impact. Instinct, he thought, must have made him drag himself towards the river, where he was found just in time by another cattleman, and taken, barely alive, to help.

"But who *is* he?" I said, still lost in thoughts of the wild horse-man. "How could a man come to be living with brumbies in the high country, a white man who knows nothing of our language or customs and who seems intent on driving us lock, stock and barrel out of the place? How could he even survive?"

"Oh, he did more than survive. He had everything he needed; food and clothing from the cattle he thieved and killed, and the command and trust of wild brumbies—who would throw the best horseman in a second—but carried him fast and freely so he could not be caught."

"But such a man could not appear from nowhere, could he?"

"That I can't say," he replied. "But there are two ways you might look at it. There's been all kinds of people pokin' around the hills over the years, from the Aborigines who were there long before us, to the prospectors and cattlemen, and the just plain ignorant who went up there in search of God knows what and perished. I know of young children who wandered away from their parents and no-one ever knew what became of them. Dead, probably, but maybe not. The natives could find a feed anywhere, moths and insects and roots where you'd think there was nothin' at all to be had, so perhaps he somehow did the same, or perhaps they took him in for a time."

"And the other way?" I said.

Old Tom took another long drink and put his mug back down. "Ah," he said. "The other way. Well, like I said, most people don't look around themselves too much, but when you're out in the bush alone and you see them stars so bright, you know there's much more. Those brumbies are new to this country, like us, but their spirit is old. We come along and push the country around, try and change it to suit ourselves, maybe there comes a time when it pushes back."

Three weeks after my meeting with Old Thomas, word came that the Talbotville Centaur, as the less reputable papers had come to call him, had been found guilty on all charges and was sentenced to hang.

I spent a lot of time trying to sort what I knew and had surmised of him into shape for a saleable story, but my thoughts kept returning to the old cattleman's tale, dragging my sympathies in two directions at once. On the one hand, there was no doubt in my mind that the man in gaol was indeed a thief and a murderer, guilty of crimes that had seen many before him mount the gibbet. But on the other . . . I had to see him once more in the flesh to settle the matter in my mind.

The next day, I made my way once again to the gaol and went through the lengthy process of gaining entry. Visitors were required to leave all possessions at the guardhouse, but on impulse I'd brought a bible with me, and this I was allowed to take in. The guard who had accompanied me on my first visit was on duty again, seeming quite cheerful.

"Not so sure this fella's ever been near a church," he said as we passed the gallows. "Oh well, the Lord moves in mysterious ways as they say, don't he?"

As before, he left me in the cell with the prisoner and went back to his station. The condemned man was crouched in his habitual position beside the wall, not looking at me, and I wondered if he could have been the one who sent Tom and his horse over the cliff, if indeed any of what the old fellow had said was true. I had no idea what I'd expected to achieve by coming there, and was overcome by a feeling of hopelessness as I studied the unkempt man who, in a few short days, would drop like a sack of wheat from the rope outside.

I lowered myself to the floor and sat cross-legged with my back against the bars. Now we were on the same level, he turned towards me and once again our gaze met. There was not the same spark of electricity as on that first day, but I felt an immense compassion for the poor fellow, a true outsider among his own species, one who could never belong in this crowded city and was perhaps better off leaving it once and for all.

I placed the bible on the floor and slid it partway across to him. What good it would do, I could not think, but there was little else I could offer. He looked from me to the leather-bound book and back again, and when our eyes met once more there was a calmness in them that had not been there a moment before. Knowing there was nothing more I could do for him, I got to my feet and called the guard.

The key clanked in the lock and the door swung open. I turned for a final look at the wretched prisoner, and just as I did so, several things happened at once. The bible was now in his hands, and he looked to me with a small jerk of his head as if telling me to move out of the way, and sprang to his feet. I reeled back as he jumped forward, swinging the heavy bible and landing a cracking blow on the guard's temple, sending him crumpling to the concrete.

The key ring still hung in the open door's lock, and I grabbed it, stepped over the unmoving guard, and took off down the corridor. After a moment's hesitation, the prisoner followed.

As we neared the guard's station, I sorted through the keys and found the one I thought opened the outer door. The coiled whip still hung on its peg and the prisoner's eyes narrowed at the sight of it. Then he went into a kind of trance, head bowed, staring at some point on the wall.

A moment later, the air was full of shouts and the whinnying and stamping of horses, followed by crashing and urgent whistle blasts. With nowhere to go but forward, I turned the key and opened the door, committing us to whatever might come next.

The yard was in uproar, with an overturned dray spilling its load onto the ground, and guards and an agitated driver ran around in pursuit of the team of horses that had been hitched to it but were now bolting around, pulling broken bits of harness behind them. Nobody noticed us at first, and my thought was to hug the walls, dodging the bedlam while making for the nearest exit.

I had run thirty yards when I sensed some change and turned back to see what was happening. Rather than following me, the prisoner had stepped out into the middle of the confusion and was standing boldly in the open. The guards, too, had realised he was there and were moving towards him with batons drawn, but as they did so, something I can still scarcely believe took place. Two of the four horses advanced on the guards, rearing and striking out with their hooves like knight's destriers, forcing the men to retreat. The other two came forward, one either side of the prisoner, and he grasped the mane of one and leapt onto its back. The other then joined its fellows and they formed a kind of shield, pushing forward while the prisoner, crouching low, was carried towards the main gate.

As he drew near, a strange sound grew from outside the prison walls, so unusual it took me a while to understand what it was; the vocalisations of innumerable horses. I could only liken it to the howling of wolves as they gave voice to their shared power.

The last I saw of the Talbotville Centaur was when he passed me, a bright elation in his eyes. He regarded me and I stared back at him. It may be foolish to ascribe meaning to that look, but if I had to swear, I would say we shared a fleeting communication as fellow primates before he was returned to his rightful place, and gone from my sight forever.

About the Author:

Tim Borella is an Australian author, mainly of short speculative fiction published in anthologies, online and in podcasts. He's also a songwriter, and has been fortunate enough to have spent most of his working life doing something he loves, flying. Tim lives with his wife Georgie in beautiful Far North Queensland, in an area recognised as the traditional lands of the Ngadjon-jii people. For more information, visit his Tim Borella – Author Facebook page.

TIM BORELLA

WEARING THE HORSE

Tamantha Smith

"I can't be responsible for all the rusting fins and dislocated wing rods." Tony looked up at Dr Meadow, expecting her to nod or give a murmur of agreeance, something to indicate he was right. But Dr Meadow looked down and concentrated on her stylus as it continued to glide over her tablet, making notes here, highlighting areas there.

"I mean . . ." Tony continued. "I never asked to be the poster-boy for mechanical re-enablements."

Dr Meadow put her stylus down and looked at Tony. Her brilliant blue eyes—*unnaturally blue*, thought Tony, *and sparkly like a tiny galaxy*—squinted at him from behind a hypnotic set of colour-changing frames. She leaned forward, allowing her silver pant suit to crinkle and shimmer in the consulting room's stark white lights. The low cut of her vest revealed her cleavage.

"Are you comfortable there, Tony?"

"What do you mean?" Tony shifted his weight a little and let his tail flick across his body. He shook the image of her breasts from his mind and tried to recall his earlier thoughts. "Comfortable as the poster boy?"

"No, Tony, on the floor. Are you comfortable on the floor?" Dr Meadow pointed to a long, padded couch—*extraordinarily long and heavily reinforced*, Tony thought, *made to fit*—by the high set of windows in her corner office. "We have arrangements for—"

Tony waited for her to say, *people like you*, or *the re-enabled*.

"—our clients," Dr Meadow said.

Tony weighed his options. The padded couch would be a much better alternative to the floor. It could support his weary frame a lot better and he wouldn't be putting so much pressure on his sternum to counterbalance the angle of his body, something his physiotherapist had been nagging him about.

It was all a matter of precision, being in this body, and it was a precision that even after three years of processing, he hadn't perfected. The readings from his hydraulics were patchy and he wasn't sure the feeble joints would cope with the bulk of his weight. He had learnt how to sit at the right angle to stop himself from squeaking on every inhale, and how to wobble his legs beneath him to reach enough velocity to stand; none of it felt as though it would be natural horse instinct and he often wondered how they had evolved into such an ungainly frame. Lifting the half ton of metal between his pelvis and the ground sometimes felt like an awful risk. He sighed and let his tail make another involuntary swipe against his body.

"No, thanks," Tony said. "I'm comfortable here."

"Why do you think you are the poster boy for re-enablements?" Dr Meadow asked, her glasses slipping as she dipped her head back to the tablet and started tapping away with her stylus once more.

"Well, I was the first, wasn't I?"

"We have been processing re-enablements for fifteen years, Tony. You weren't our first re-enabled client."

"You know what I mean, doctor. I was the first like this," Tony said, pointing to his hindquarters, his hooves, his irregularly flicking tail. "The first human-animal cyborg."

Tony remembered the procedure from the early days, the searing pain that happened every time his nerves fired, sending signals to his cybernetic half, and the signals rebounding back, confused and irritated. It took months of physical therapy to learn how to make the motors in his hindquarters kick in and how to make a single step. It wasn't the same as learning how to roll and stop a wheelchair with your hands; there was a lot of brain power involved and it drove him to headaches and overwhelming fatigue. Most of the time he just felt dumb, and the doctors around him seemed to feel the same. Tony often heard them saying that they had "picked the wrong candidate".

"Yes," Dr Meadow said. "You were the first to undertake inter-species re-enablement. As I understand, the procedure was voluntary. Were you not offered standard limb attachments?"

"They offered them to me, with a hefty price tag too. Disability payments wouldn't cover that. But, c'mon doctor, who's going to take something as regular as that, when they said I could be a racehorse, jockey and all?"

Dr Meadow hmphed and slid her glasses back onto her nose.

"Hung like a horse, they reckon, but I wouldn't know. I can't see down there. I don't feel much movement. Honestly, I'm not sure they even programmed that part in. It wasn't in the brochure, that's for sure." Tony laughed.

Dr Meadow didn't laugh. Instead, she uncrossed her legs, and recrossed them. Her silver pant suit sent brilliant sparkles throughout the room and into Tony's eyes, forcing him to blink.

"It was fun at first. And I can't say I didn't enjoy the attention." Tony rubbed at his eyes forcing back irritated tears. "It was better than being that bloke in the wheelchair, begging for a spot in the elevator or trying to bridge the gap between the train and the station. If I need people to move now, they move."

"People notice you now. There's a power to that, isn't there?" Dr Meadow asked.

"Yeah, I guess so." Tony sat a little higher, his hindquarters groaning and squealing as he moved.

"People pay to come see me stand on a stage, to talk to them about re-enablements and the . . . uh . . . fantasy elements that can be built in. I'm no expert though, they should be talking to doctors like you, but instead they ask me, and they get so angry when I don't have answers for them. Look at these, doctor."

Tony twisted to the small satchel on his side. His horse frame wobbled as he adjusted to an unsettled equilibrium. He dusted off a small tablet and offered it to Dr Meadow.

"What am I looking at, Tony?"

"Read 'em. You'll see why I . . . well, why I came back for this today."

Dr Meadow skimmed the first email.

Dear Tony,

You're my idol. Ever since I first saw you step (trot, haha!) onto that stage in Brisbane, I knew I wanted to be like you. My wheelchair was the pits and I could never afford a lower body re-enablement. The discount animal stuff was perfect. There was a time, when I was little, where you could hardly pull me from the ocean. I would swim and squeal and daydream of being a mermaid!

Problem is, Tony, my scales and fins are rusting in the water. I don't have the money to pay for the regular check-ups anymore. Is there some way you know to stop me from rusting? I'm afraid to go back in the water and now I'm back in the wheelchair to get around. People look at me funny and I have to cover my tail with a blanket. I guess a fish was a stupid choice.

Anyway, I know you're busy.

Phoebe

And the next . . .

Hello Tony!

I have been watching your progress from the start. I think it's amazing that you're a centaur. Do you have Greek in you? Did you choose it from those old myths?

Anyway, what I really want to ask is about the re-enablements. I went for the budget animal option because full arm re-enablements weren't in my insurance plan. It was a tough choice, but I looked at you and said, "Follow your dreams, Palmer". I have wings instead of hands. They're okay but I have been trying to twist the feathers the way I would a hand and some things have busted. The doctors say it's some important wing rods and I can't fly anymore or pick things up.

I am probably asking the wrong person because I know work on humans on the black market can land a person in jail, but do you know anyone that can fix these rods for me?

Someone a bit cheaper than the proper docs? If they're here in Victoria, even better!

Run fast, you glorious stallion!

Palmer Wyatt

The last was prefaced with a series of angry red exclamation marks.

Tony,

You have completely fucked me over. That's the last time I ever listen to you. "You could do more guys at a time with eight of those hands, like an octopus", you said. "That's eight times as much coin," you said. I didn't even need re-enabling, you daft prick!

Octopus tentacles! Who the fuck gets octopus tentacles ADDED to their existing limbs? While they hit the mark—you know what I mean—no one ever explained they came with jet black ink that squirted at inappropriate moments. The doctors claim that's a malfunction, coz even normal octopuses don't squirt ink through their tentacles, but I do. They can't fix me, though, without a big fucking payment, and they're not keen on testing the tentacles because of the whole ink issue, so I'm right fucked, aren't I?

Good old joke, Tony.

The Needy Pearl has a big poster of you with 'No Re-enabled!' on it now. Don't ever show your face around here again or you'll be getting that ink.

Livvy

"Well . . ." Dr Meadow started.

"That last one, I probably messed with a little. Would be pretty interesting, eh? Squirting ink like that everywhere. That's got to be better than being an awkward half-horse. But those stories, they're the reason why I don't want to be the poster boy anymore. I don't want them thinking I screwed them over. I mean, I got lots of money from all of this, but it's not enough to help them all out, you know. I can't just give it all away. A man's still got to look out for himself."

Dr Meadow cleared her throat, placed her tablet on the table beside her and stood. "Tony, I am not here to counsel you on your decision. I am merely here to check your vitals, which are fine, apart from some slack to the hind joints, and a heart that has a slightly odd rhythm. I also need to confirm that this—" Dr Meadow strode to the furthest corner and pulled a sheet from a standing display to reveal two shiny pairs of humanoid legs, "—is what you paid for."

Each leg was fitted with next generation metalloids that were both flexible and hyper-strengthened; embedded with the most advanced cybernetics. New parts were expensive, and these legs were years' worth of savings. Years of parading a fly-swatting, clunky horse hide to crowds of amputees. Tony nodded. *Worth it.*

"That's them!" Tony's eyes glittered. "Lightning fast they reckon. About as fast as these horse legs once were, but better, coz no one will recognise me. Put on a pair of pants, and—poof!—I'm just like everyone else. No more being a sucker in a subsidised horse suit."

"Sign this," Dr Meadow said, thrusting the tablet at Tony. "The procedure will take about two days with monitored recovery. This form gives us permission to reuse the old hindquarters."

"Pfft. Okay. But what kind of chump would seriously want these old creaking joints, the stink of fake horse hair and a tail that just doesn't let up?" Tony scoffed, scrawling a signature on the dotted line.

"Jacob. He's seven. He lost his legs six weeks ago and his family is uninsured. Luckily, he wants to be just like his hero, Tony."

About the Author:

Tamantha Smith is an emerging Australian writer of speculative fiction, currently living in Jarowair country, Queensland. She reviews for Aurealis magazine while studying for her Bachelor of Arts (Honours) in Creative and Critical Writing with USQ, working full time in the Royal Australian Navy, and supporting her crazy little family of four.

Tamantha is a passionate introvert that spends half her life inside her own head imagining the future in all its possible woe and glory.

Nunki's Arrows

Nikky Lee

I was seven centuries old when my gift revealed itself. A mere foal by godling standards. But in that time I'd seen Chiron unlock the talents of heroes; studied how he'd drawn out Achilles' courage, Heracles' strength and Jason's cunning and released them into the world. Men and gods alike called Chiron *The Wisest, The Justest*. I knew him by another name.

Father.

Nunki, he called me. He never said why. But then, he never said much. He hoarded words as a merchant hoards silver. Spent not a syllable more than he needed to. Besides, first names weren't important to godlings. The name bestowed when a gift revealed itself was the one that mattered. The one you were remembered for. And the day my gift came, when I should have received my new name and taken up my calling, he died.

Godlings are not immortal like the true gods. We can be wounded. We can be slain. We can be poisoned. My father was all three. A poison arrow in the end. Right through the foot.

"Don't be sorry," he'd whispered as I wept over him and at what I'd done.

My sisters and brother blamed Heracles—Father's mentee and favourite hero—who'd returned to us the night before flush with his victory over the hydra. Heracles blamed himself and his drunkenness for dropping a hydra spine on his teacher's foot.

But that's not what happened. I remember like it was yesterday. As for my gift, well, that had surprised father and I both.

"My gift is to have no gift."

My siblings stared at me aghast, like I'd not so much as grown an extra head but lost my only one. A godling without a gift. I was a perversion. A snake without its skin; a fish without gills. We were simply not made that way.

"Unthinkable," Melanippe had said, dark curls brushing her shoulders as she shook her head.

"It can't be," fair Carystus insisted. "You tried music? Father always had skill for a tune, perhaps you do too."

It had taken a butchered melody on a lyre to convince him otherwise.

Mute Ocyrhoe had rested a hand on my collar and stared mournfully into my face, her auburn hair haloed in a tangle around her head. Of all my siblings, I loved her the most. Hers was the gift of listening, she could hear across the world with it. But in the way of gifts, it was a double-edged sword; she'd not spoken a word in centuries. The secrets she learned stayed secret.

"It's okay, I'm all right with it," I'd said to her.

Her brown eyes considered me a long moment, and for a horrible heartbeat I thought she knew. That she'd been listening close to home the day Father died. But then she sighed and cupped my cheek as if to say *I'm sorry.*

So I remained Nunki, the unremarkable. The forgotten. Not banished, just left to my own devices. No pressure to breed heroes or wise men, no expectation to live up to the legacy of Chiron's blood in my veins. I withdrew to the edge of our realm and was content to fall into obscurity. A fitting punishment, I thought, for killing my own father.

Imagine my surprise when the first human sought me out in my cave at the foot of Mount Olympus. She was no hero, thin and bony like she'd slept rough for nights untold and skipped more meals than she'd eaten. From the look on her face—caught between shock and weariness—she hadn't expected to find me, of all creatures, here.

73

A knife flashed into her hand, the blade worn and flecked with rust. "Who are you?" she demanded.

I uncurled myself from my bed of reeds, and as I came close, her face paled. She gripped the knife tighter.

"What are you?" she amended.

That, I'd thought, was a little unfair. True, I was taller and broader than her, but that wasn't saying much. I wasn't *that* different—apart from the fur-tipped ears, the faint whorl of horsehair on my forehead and the two branches that curled from my brow. I'd always taken after my dryad mother. I was a dryad in nearly every sense but one: my gift.

"I am Nunki," I said.

The knife relaxed a little, a disbelieving look creeping over that scrawny face. "*You're* Nunki?"

I faltered. "You know of me?" Impossible. I'd not ventured into the mortals' cities, nor ever spoken to any travellers or hunters who had crossed into my woods.

"Artemis sent me." The girl put her knife away, suddenly matter-of-fact. "She said you'd train me."

Artemis. I ground the name out under my breath, cursing her in five languages. The goddess and I had crossed paths once or twice, but I'd never thought she'd ever *send* someone to me.

"Why?" I asked. "I'm no teacher."

"She said you were," the girl replied as she seated herself at my table. "Said you had a gift for killing."

I went still, the breath clogging in my lungs. *How?* How could Artemis *know?* But then Artemis is a God of the wilds, she could have heard it from a songbird, or a bug, for all I knew.

The girl grinned—a gaunt thing, all teeth and hollow cheeks. "I want you to teach me."

"*Teach* you?"

"There's a king who needs killing."

She'd been a gardener once, in a kingdom far south, she told me. From a family of gardeners. Her mother and grandmother before her. It had been hard but honest work and the royal family had been good to them. Until the birth of the prince.

"Mother said he was born with something missing," the girl explained over supper. "As a child, I'd find dead birds in the palace flowerbeds. Their heads gone; legs broken. I thought it was the royal cat until I found the cat the same way." She gave a hollow laugh. "If only that had been as far as it went."

She'd found a finger next. Skin loose and joints swollen with age. Lopped off above the knuckle.

"It was like he was teasing me, planting his bloody flowers in the garden where he knew I'd find them." Her hands squeezed into fists as she spoke. "Mother slapped me something good when I told her about the prince and what I'd found. 'Hold your tongue or you'll end us all!' she'd said."

The girl had still been young. Still thought her mother knew best. And she'd heard the fear laced in her mother's words. So, she'd obeyed. When she'd found more body parts—an ear, a thumb, a toe, all of them old and withered in the garden outside the prince's rooms—she'd cleared them away without a word.

Then she'd found a whole hand. This one young and supple. Slender fingers with calluses on their tips, those of a musician. And she recalled that one of the palace bards had gone missing two days before. Who'd last been seen entering the prince's chambers.

"We should have left then. When the old king sickened, I begged mother and father to leave," the girl said, staring into the hearth as I brewed tea. "But when the king died, we were still there. And then *he* took the throne, and it became so much worse."

Instead of parts, she found bodies. In the space of a month her family went from gardeners to grave diggers.

"I even found the queen's page boy dead under a tower window," she said. "His body was broken a hundred ways and not all of them from the fall."

She'd thought that had been the worst of it until her mother went missing. The girl stalled there, unable to finish as her face crumpled into a mess of grief. She slammed her skinny fist on my table. "We should have fled!" she repeated through her tears. "I should have made them see sense. If only we had run."

"Hindsight is a cruel knowing," I replied. How many times had I wished I'd known what I know now of my gift before I'd presented myself to my father for a naming? How excited I'd been to feel the knowledge open in my mind like a rose—of woods and metals, blades and fletching. It had not so much sprung forth from nothing, more that a particular set of learnings from my centuries under Chiron's tutelage had suddenly come together and woven themselves into a gift.

"A forger's gift. It's a sound hypothesis." Father had stroked his beard, pleased when I'd come running to him. "But you must demonstrate its validity before I give you your name."

If only I'd known then what I know now. That my hypothesis had been wrong. In all my eagerness, I'd not considered the alternatives. That my gift might not be to forge mere weapons, but death itself. And when I'd handed death to him, so lovingly and unknowingly crafted, Father's face had contorted from expectation into horror. If I close my eyes, I see him snatch his hand from the bow I'd made him. I see my poison arrow tumble through the air, end over end, and bury into his foot, laying him low.

Had I known then what I know now, Father would still be alive.

I considered the girl weeping at my table. Considered what and all she asked. This was not a job for heroes, and I couldn't make her into one. But perhaps I could turn her into something else.

"I will help you," I said at last.

I had no idea where to start. But start we did. Slowly at first. Trial and error. Me stretching out my gift's knowledge for the first time in decades, rigorously testing every skill before passing it on. Her, building up her strength, her stealth, her knowing of plants and poisons and her skill with the blade and bow.

Three years she was with me. Three years of forging her into a weapon to strike down a king. And in that forging she named herself anew: Arrow.

When she was ready, I loosed her into the heart of her enemy.

I never saw her again. Though I did hear tell of the sudden death of King Tiernat in the south, brought down by an unknown foe, and I was glad. Not for a second did think I'd wake to a knocking on my cave door early one morning to find a one-armed, one-eyed man there.

"I'm told you can help me," he said, and he told me his tale. A merchant had stolen him as a teen, sailed him across the sea and sold him to a fighting ring. Twelve years he'd fought and bled, and at last he had escaped to search for the merchant who had stolen his life.

"How did you hear of me?" I asked.

The man shrugged. "I had a dream. It told me to come here and ask the help of the first person I met."

First Artemis and now Morpheus, God of Dreams. Safe to say my gift was no longer my closely held secret. The thought was not as upsetting as I thought it would be. I'd never expected to keep the secret forever. But that didn't stop the little quiver of fear ripple over my skin at the thought of Melanippe, Carystus and Ocyrhoe learning the truth.

Fletch, my second student named himself. Rough on the edges, but he'd still fly true. His body was already honed, if a bit battered. So I went to work on his mind. I filled it with plants and poisons, alchemy and traps. Five years he learned under me; his mind flexing in its new-found strength. Clever turned to cunning. Knack to knowledge. Scheming to strategy. If it weren't for his vengeance, he might have become a politician—or a warlord. Perhaps he did after. I do not know.

That is the hard thing about these stories. I never know how they end. I'm left to listen to the tales each new guest brings and guess the rest.

Not that my effort with Fletch went unreciprocated.

"You have my gratitude, Nunki," he said on his final day. "Word in the mortal cities is that your father was the finest teacher to ever walk these lands. While I was never his student, I was yours. And I'd wager you are as finer teacher as he."

I laughed. "I'm no teacher." I looked up to the stars to where Zeus had placed Father after his death. Forever out of reach. "Father set heroes forth into the world while I . . ." I trailed off, not wanting to insult my student and friend on his final day. *While I set loose killers. Living weapons forged in my gift and sent across the world into the hearts of other men.*

Fletch flashed me a look through his one good eye, not fooled for a second. "Perhaps weapons are what the world needs. To strike down the evil in it. Is that not what the heroes do, in their own way?"

I frowned, thinking I'd schooled him too well in rhetoric. Yet, his reasoning stuck in my mind. "I've never thought of it like that," I admitted.

"Perhaps it's time you do," Fletch suggested. "You are not just *like* an archer, you *are* one. Your quiver is the people you teach, your range the world over." He pointed to the constellation above us. "Your father may have been the world's finest teacher, but you are its finest archer."

The weight of his last word sank in, tingling in my bones. And like that, I came to know my name.

Archer.

Which brings me to the third. She was special. I found her as a babe, all brown eyed and fawn-soft locks that melted through my fingers. Her mother was with me a single night before she succumbed to the rent in her belly. Bandits had taken a liking to my woods. And when the mother breathed her last, I closed her eyes and collected my quiver from my hearthside. I threw open my door, nocked my arrows, aimed at the stars and fired. One after another.

I trusted my gift to do the rest.

The next day I found an abandoned camp. Five bodies lay struck down in the earth—arrows in their backs and chests.

I named the babe Nock. And she grew ravenously. Despite my time with Fletch and Arrow, I'd never truly realised how fleeting mortal life is. Or how fast they grow. One day I was brewing a sleeping potion, eyes raw from sleepless nights, head in a daze; anything to get the dratted child to settle. The next, she was high as my hip and I was running after her, yelling for her to put on her Zeus-damn shoes before playing outside.

She was a wild thing. With so many brambles snagged in her hair she looked more the dryad than I. She was no good at sitting still. But she took to the blade like she'd been born with one in her hand. She loved stories, particularly ones of the heroes my father had taught.

In a mere blink she was fifteen going on sixteen. And restless.

81

"Have you ever thought about leaving the forest?" she asked.

"Why would I? We have everything we need here."

Nock pursed her lips, not satisfied with my answer. "Haven't you ever wondered what else is out there?"

I shrugged and continued slicing roots for a stew. "Not especially."

She flipped her knife around her knuckles—a showy movement I had never taught her—and heaved a sigh. A bit overwrought, but she was young. "Could we not go? A short trip." A quick grin. "You might find you like it out there."

"Absolutely not." We weren't adventurers, we didn't do those things. And Nock's suggestion chilled me to the bone. The thought of Arrow or Fletch's stories befalling her sent my heart pelting into my ribs. No, she was safe here. Where I was with her. Yes, I was a coward through and through.

Nock's face fell. "But why?"

I snatched the knife from her knuckles as she made to flick it again. With the blade gripped loose in my fingers, I waggled the handle under her nose. "Because I am your mother and I say so."

She blew out her cheeks and snatched the knife back. I let her take it. "No playing—"

"—with knives at the table, I know," she finished.

That was not the end of it. All through summer she nagged and begged, debated and cajoled. Winter gave us a brief reprieve, but as soon as the first buds of spring opened, she was back at it.

"I'm going," she announced one day, as I'd feared she might. "You can't stop me."

I could, but with my gift it could turn deadly, and I didn't want that. Couldn't even bear the thought of hurting her. Or her me. She'd long ago learned everything I could teach her. It was what I couldn't teach her that worried me.

"Be careful, promise me," I said, hugging her tight at the edge of the forest. Nock held me for a moment, then wormed out of my grip and flicked her knife again.

Who, it occurred to me to think then, *had taught her that?* Why had I not thought to ask earlier?

By that point, it was too late. My mortal child had already raced down the road, her pack bouncing on her back, knifes swinging on her belt. And there, on the rise that parted my forest from the world beyond, she paused, turned, and waved. Once. Her lips moved. I was too far to hear but I thought they shaped out, "I'll be back soon."

I hoped they did.

So I returned to my cave. Strangely quiet it was. Still beyond measure. I lit the hearth and busied myself with supper. Then onto sweeping the floors, preparing herbs, sharpening knives. The last blade of my set honed and gleaming, I held it up to the firelight and said, without thinking, "What a pretty blade, don't you think?"

The silence that answered cut deeper than any knife.

I slept poorly that night, tossing and turning on my reeds. *She's fine. She'll be fine,* I told myself over and over. Those words turned into a mantra as the days wore on, and I'd almost believed them until Ocyrhoe knocked on my door late one evening.

"Sister!" I exclaimed, delighted to see her. I showed her in, fussed about with my hearth and pot for tea. How long had it been? Decades? Centuries? But when I handed Ocyrhoe a cup of steeped herbs, her expression was all wrong. Lips tight. Brow creased. Eyes earnest. There was no joy there. But concern. Dread even.

The pot slipped from my fingers and smashed against the floor. "It's Nock, isn't it?" My voice shook.

A nod.

I swallowed. "She's in danger?"

Another nod.

"From who? The gods?" My fists clenched. If Zeus or any of his sons had laid a finger on her I'd—but Ocyrhoe shook her head. I sucked in a breath and fought down panic. "Godlings?"

My sister hesitated, then dipped her chin. Affirmative.

My heart turned over. Gooseflesh prickled up my arms. I didn't want to ask. I knew the answer as sure as the heat of the hearth burning at my back. "*Our* family?"

Another nod and she dipped one finger in her tea and attempted to scrawl a name on my table. Her gift cramped up her arm after the first letter, such was her curse: to listen and know, but never to tell. Not directly. Ocyrhoe hissed under her breath and shook out her fingers, exasperated. I stared at the wet smear on the wood. One letter but it was enough for me to put the rest together.

"Melanippe?"

I could think of only one reason why a godling, why my eldest sister would dare go after Nock. Vengeance. The truth about Father's death had finally found its way to her.

Ocyrhoe's hand caught mine and she stared into my face. *I'm sorry*, she mouthed.

My fingers squeezed hers tight. "This is not your sorrow to bear. It's mine." I should have told them. Should have owned up to what I'd done. But my gift had been young and new and terrifying. I'd been afraid of what I could do. Of what I might be made to do. And the guilt. So thick and heavy it had dragged on my limbs like chains.

So I'd slunk away. Fled from all the reminders of what I'd done. A tingle washed over me. I could not go on hiding. Not with Nock in danger.

I straightened. "Where is my daughter?"

Ocyrhoe took my hand and led me out through the trees; her hooved feet leaving little imprints on the grass. She led me to a chestnut horse tethered to a low-slung tree branch. One look and I recognised Pegasus' seed. Hard to ignore the wings sprouting from the mount's shoulders or the way those hooves barely touched the earth—like the creature was made of cloud. But when I rested a hand against his flank, he was solid and real under my fingers.

"Where did you find him?" I asked, forgetting myself.

Ocyrhoe lips curled into a faint smile. *A gift,* she mouthed. *From Carystus.*

Our brother always did have a taste for fine things. I ran a hand down the horse's neck and its baleful eyes swung to me and it whickered a greeting. Ocyrhoe pressed the reins into my hands.

"No, Ocyrhoe, I can't take him."

She waggled her finger and took my hand, miming me returning the reins to her. The message was clear. Not take. Borrow. The matter apparently settled, Ocyrhoe lifted a finger and pointed due West.

"That way, is it?" My stomach clenched at the thought of what I might find. I mounted the steed—Kallias I called him in my head. *Beautiful.*

There is very little you can do on a flying horse but watch the earth pass beneath you. Kallias did his job, and he did it well. Carried me a day and a night to the fortress of Chyton, deep in the lands of Epirus.

Blood awaited me there. Flecked on the marble pillars in drying shades. I unsheathed my knife and I pressed through the pillars, half expecting shadows to shift to swinging blades. This was the world of humans, godlings didn't belong here. There was a reason why we trained heroes to do our work rather than do it ourselves. We can be killed, we can be slain, and we can be poisoned. And the world of humans is full of fatal possibilities. I never said I was the only coward.

And you let Nock come here without even putting up a fight. I clenched my knife and hurried on.

That's when I heard it. A soft, almost inaudible crying. The faintest sniff of a nose, a wiping of the eyes, then a ragged breath. I followed it. Around a corner, down a passage, and into . . . into . . .

Horror.

The smell hit me first. It hung in the air, thick enough to swallow, every breath a gulp of iron and dank earth. Then my eyes found the bodies. Dozens of them. Throats opened, femoral arteries slashed at the thigh, axillary arteries punctured under the arm. All of them armed, their spears and bronze swords scattered to the floor.

A knot folded in my belly. *Please no.*

Another sob. I spun.

There she was. My Nock. My arrow. Rocking back and forth, hugging a fallen figure in her arms. It was a young man, a few years older than she. Tall. Muscular. Curls for hair—and the gold wreath of a hero resting within them.

The knot in my gut wretched. A hero. There was only one place they trained those.

In a heartbeat, it all made sense. Her insistence on leaving our den to see the world. Her excitement on the day of her leaving. The knife trick I hadn't taught her.

"Oh Nock."

At the sound of my voice, my daughter straightened, peeled herself from her dead lover's body. Her eyes were wide and stricken, dried blood crusted in her hair.

"It just happened," she began. "I couldn't stop." Her eyes roved the massacre, seeing and not seeing. I recognised the look. I had once done the same with Father's death. Reliving the moment again and again, trying to figure out when it had all gone wrong.

I swept Nock into my arms and held her.

"I'm sorry, I'm sorry," she whispered over and over. Whether to me or the dead boy at her feet I couldn't say.

"Hush, it's not your fault," I said. The wrong words to say.

"But it is! All of it," Nock choked, and when I tried to steer her away from the carnage, she wouldn't budge. Her fingers gripped her lover's tunic so tight her nails cut into her palms through the fabric. For a second time I took in the body, noticing the knife embedded in his throat, expertly angled into the carotid artery. One of Nock's knives.

"I k-killed him." Nock shook in my arms. "It was *me*. I couldn't stop. Couldn't—"

I eased her grip from the hero's tunic, finger by finger. Rubbed her hands in mine. They were slick and sticky.

A tittering laugh rang from the end of the hall.

"Oh my, isn't this an endearing scene."

There was no need to turn. After seven centuries living with her, I knew her voice. "Melanippe," I acknowledged, rising. "This is your doing?"

My eldest sister strode through the bodies, the strike of her hooves on the marble hard and grating. Of all Chiron's children, she resembled our father most. Thin face, pointed chin, dark hair pulled into a warrior's braid. Like Father, her olive-smooth torso tapered into an equine body. But unlike Father, hers was all fury and pent-up energy. She was a creature born to run, to fight. Her muscles quivered as she approached, taut as a flexed bow string. A child born to all of my father's power, and none of his calm. Her gift of storms suited her well.

My fingers found the hilt of my dagger in my belt.

"All I did was give a little push," Melanippe said. "A lover to woo her here and a one hundred drachma reward to the man who claimed your daughter's head. Your dear Nock did the rest." Her eyes turned on the scene, landing on Nock still cradling the dead hero. "And what a mess it is." Her lips split open in delight. "I mean, I knew you'd forge her as you did the others, but for you to turn an innocent into such a *killer* is—" she clapped her hands together "—extraordinary."

I scowled. "Your grievance was with me, sister. Not my daughter."

Melanippe pouted her bottom lip. "All I wanted was to test my niece a little. And she was just so *fond* of my new hero." Her gaze paused on the dead boy. "A shame she killed him in her frenzy. He had some promise. Even if he ignored my instructions to leave her alone when my soldiers came. Not to worry, there will be others."

I closed my eyes, imagining his terror as Nock's instincts took over. The horror as Melanippe's trap swung shut and he realised what they'd woken.

My gaze dropped to the bodies again. I'd noted their armour when I'd entered but had not seen the shields buried among them. These were hoplites—trained soldiers—a whole phalanx of them. I lifted the edge of an upturned shield of the nearest one and glimpsed a blood-streaked crest embossed into the metal. Father's crest: the shape of his constellation emblazoned in bronze.

"You sacrificed them," I said, not quite believing it. Melanippe had always been cold, but I'd never known her to be cruel. "Sacrificed your own hero."

"Like you sacrificed Father," Melanippe spat. "You were the one who struck him dead Nunki, do not presume to lecture me!"

My hands shook as I clenched them at my side. No running from the truth anymore. "That was an accident."

Melanippe snorted, her glare turning my gut over. "Really, Nunki? You're still clinging to that lie? After all this?" She spread her arms to the dead. "A gift only works when you will it. You wanted Father dead. But what drove you to it? That he spent more time attending his precious *heroes* than you?" she sneered. "That he scolded you for not being as clever as Jason or strong as Heracles, or brave as Achilles?"

"Your words, not mine, Melanippe." I gripped Nock by the shoulders and pulled her to her feet, heedless of how her lover flopped to the floor in his own blood and excrement. "Come," I whispered to her. "Let's go home."

Nock's face remained slack, her eyes unfocused, locked in some dark dream I couldn't break.

"That's right, go back and cower in your hole, Nunki," Melanippe hissed. "Your daughter won't recover. She slew her lover, Nunki."

Her words had such venom, so much hatred, that I could only stop and stare. This was not the sister I knew. Where was the girl who'd run to the Aegean and back just to prove she could? Who'd loved with a fierce, unbridled passion, and would brush off a scolding like it was a bit of dust? Where was the wild girl I'd grown up with; the woman I'd known when I'd withdrawn in my shame? My stomach twisted.

Had I caused this?

I stood frozen before Melanippe, heart and thoughts racing. Nausea crawled up my throat and I clutched Nock to hold myself steady. I could not fall apart here. Nock needed me. And yet the thoughts circled vicious in my head. *You did this. You killed him. You abandoned them.*

Why? I wanted to cry. Why didn't you come to me, Melanippe? We could have talked. Even though I'd been the one who'd left, who had shunned all contact.

But to go as far as targeting Nock. To take her vengeance on my innocent girl . . . My dagger jerked free with a will of its own. I could have thrown it, let it sail true into Melanippe's throat. End that sad creature in a sure blow. I wanted to. Longed to. My body shook with it. Every fibre longed to shunt my blade deep in her chest for what she'd done. One step was all it would take. One lunge and a swift cut to her unprotected neck.

I shoved my dagger back into my belt. I was not a slave to my gift. Not anymore. Enough blood had spilled today. And more than enough grief.

Hands shaking, I took Nock's wrist and led her away.

Melanippe's eyes followed us. *This is my vengeance. For what you did to Father. For what you did to me.* The words hung in the air between us as if she'd screamed them.

"I'll never forgive you." She spoke low and angry, without triumph. Dead inside.

Those are the last words she said to me. They will haunt me forever.

When I glanced back, Melanippe had gone. She didn't see the tears that fell as I made my way back to Kallias and took Nock to the only place that could help her.

Kallias's hooves sank into the muddy bank of the River Lethe. Above, the tall arch of a limestone cavern crested—a wave of stone poised over our heads, its surface twinkling with glow worms. A faint lap of water sounded from the darkness across the cavern. Float a skiff into that black and you'd find your way to the Underworld.

Gently, I eased Nock from the saddle. She came numbly, her face still blank with the shock, and she moved hunched over and shuffling, as if she had aged overnight.

"Are you hurt anywhere?" I asked, cursing myself for not thinking it sooner.

"No," Nock whispered.

"Good." I set her down on the bank and took her hands in mine. Her fingers were stiff too, from fighting or clutching her dead hero it was hard to say. "Nock, listen to me. I want to give you a choice."

Her head lifted, watery eyes turning on me; the things she'd done mirrored in them.

A sob gathered in my chest. "This is the River Lethe." I motioned to the water. "If you want, you may drink from it. One sip. Just one. Then you will forget."

A long pause and Nock stared at the water. "All of it?" she asked.

"Everything," I said. "The pain, the blood, the killing. You won't remember any of it. Only," I hesitated, "you won't remember me either. Or anything of our time together."

My daughter studied me, a slow horror drawing her out of her numbness. "No, Nunki, I can't." A flicker of temper, just a flicker. Like a tiny flame of a candle sputtering in a storm. "How could you even suggest it?" She shook her head. "No."

94

Her flame wasn't snuffed out, not yet. And Gods be damned, I wasn't going to let it die. I caught Nock's chin and held it gently in my fingertips. "Think about what happened," I say. "It will be with you as long as you live. It will come to you in every quiet minute. When you close your eyes, it will follow you into your dreams. Can you learn to live with it?"

Nock quivered in my grasp. Her eyes turned distant again, reliving the horror of the gift I'd bestowed on her without her asking. Her lips trembled. Tears welled in her eyes. "I don't . . ." she floundered. "I can't . . . I . . . I'm sorry, Nunki." And like that she dissolved into me, holding me tight through her sobs.

I hugged her back and stroked her hair. "Don't be sorry." Father's words echoed through me, and I finally understood what he'd meant. I was the one who should be sorry, not my child. Not the girl who'd been too young to understand the power I'd taught her. I motioned to Lethe's waters.

"Drink this and you can have a life. A good life. Full of joy and laugher and love." *And you can be a woman, not a weapon,* I wanted to add. That was my shame to bear. My mistake. One on a long list.

Nock stilled in my arms. "You'll stay with me?" she asked. "Until . . ."

"I will," I promised. "And when you wake, you will be somewhere better. Somewhere safe, where there's hope and happiness."

"I'd like that," Nock swallowed, and slowly—as if it pained her—she nodded. "All right. But give me one thing."

"Anything."

"Help me choose a new name."

We chose Elpida. *Hope.* I scored it on her palm with my knife so she would see it when she woke—and would continue to see if for years to come. Then I cupped my hands to the River Lethe's waters and brought them to her mouth. One sip, no more. Nock laid her head on my lap and shut her eyes, her hand tight around mine until Lethe's sleep claimed her.

I took her to Delphi and left her in the care of the oracles there. As advisors to kings and the great families, they knew the world of mortals better than I. Who better to teach my daughter how to find her way in it? I never returned. Though, the oracles assured me in their letters that she grew into a delightful woman, brash and defiant and full of life. She lived well, they said.

She's bones in the earth now.

And so concludes my tale and brings me to yours. You've sought me out, heard my story. You've heard that in Arrow I learned my gift, in Fletch my name, and in Nock. . . in Nock I learned that my gift is not for everyone. This is a power you must choose, and you must be willing to bear its weight. It is why I tell all my acolytes this story. I will not see innocence destroyed like that again.

Now it is your turn. Come, sit at my table. You have been a long time travelling.

Speak, stranger and tell me your story.

Tell me who you wish to kill.

For only then will I judge if you are fit to join my quiver.

About the Author:

Nikky grew up as a barefoot 90s child in Perth, Western Australia, before moving to New Zealand in 2016. By day she works as a professional content writer and by night authors speculative fiction, often burning the candle at both ends to explore fantastic worlds, mine asteroids and meet wizards. Her creative work has appeared in magazines, on radio and in anthologies around the world. Her debut novel, The Rarkyn's Familiar—*a dark tale of a girl bonded to a monster—will be published by Parliament House Press in 2022.*

You can find her online at:
W:nikkythewriter.com | T:@NikkyMLee | F:nikkythewriter

THE HIGHWAY

Georgia MacShane

In the stories, the songs, they say flowers grow in the cracks where blood is spilt. All kinds of blood. Every night—once the sun disappears behind those razor-cut mountains and the hitchhikers become silent in their ditches—the animals come out and, on the highway, feast.

Coyotes stalk through the valleys and pass cacti; eagles catch the moon on their wing tips as they descend. Rattlesnakes hiss, slithering beside desert rats. Some in the west claim jackalopes, but others stick to what they can swear they've seen. All these creatures feasting on the flowers, ripping them from the crevices, frenzy in their eyes, bellies swollen. Then they fight.

The rest stop was miles in my rear-view mirror, giving comfort with each passing minute. I threw the last cigarette I had stolen out the window and became content.

A rabbit's head in a coyote's jaw, a snake wrapping around an eagle, rats turning on each other. Blood spilling on the highway, draining into the asphalt cracks. In the morning, more flowers would grow, only to be crushed by an onslaught of cars, torn by bitter winds, or choked by brittle bush and dandelion root.

They say if you pick them up, your fingers are stained ruby red under your nails, in the lines of your worn palms.

Your eyes, I won't forget those. Your touch, either. It lingers on my cheek, my neck, my feet. My gaze flickers to the side mirror, along my jaw lies your kiss.

The question is always asked at this point. Why do they fight? Why is it this place? There is no reason, nothing to say to possibly understand these wild, feral laws of nature. The eagle pecks at bodies amongst the rocks, stealing strands of a dead love's golden hair for a nest. That same eagle will rot on them when it one day drops dead from the sky. Maybe we are born from the earth only to return to it.

The road is stained forever, by animals, teenagers, lovers, gangsters, outlaws. Years ago, but still today.

The young ones sit on stolen suitcases, their weary sneakers on the edge of the road, laces sticking to the melted tar. Dust on their tongues and desperation in their eyes, taking a chance on stained leather seats and tinted windows. Only to be wrapped in plastic to embrace the earth, eyes fixed to heaven, the last scream an echo on their lips. Another to the highway, never to be seen again.

I shivered when I first heard the stories about this place. It hadn't stopped the pull I felt, how I feel it now as I drive.

Speeding in cars, clouds of vodka coughed into the night air. Everything so fast, so fantastic. Soft spoken crooners on their scratchy radios, then Elvis on cracked cassettes, *Tiny Dancer* on 8-tracks lined with grease. Laughing and smiling, feeling alive, invincible. Skidding on the smallest oil patch, careening into a cactus with roots that burrow far under the sand. Blood dripping down fingers, into fractures in the road. The cycle continues.

The bleeding still hasn't stopped. The tissue from the truck stop used and gone, now it's soaking into my cotton dress. The blood spreading across the fibres. The sun is still too high overhead—I must drive on.

Perfume-soaked song girls and cut-throat cowboys; playing with fire, rolling the dice. Taking chances and losing. Living their life by gunfire. Damning souls with double crosses and ill-fated last stands. Broken fingers and crushed cages from corsets, downing illegal liquor shots that swish with the disease in their livers. Wounds getting deeper, hearts getting broken. Lovers rolling them up in carpets—the nicest ones—and leaving them along the highway. Rains wash sand and soil over them in the wet season, the carpets now buried in a mocking barrow. Flowers growing over and blooming. Again and again.

Those souls are still there, trapped along the road. Visible when headlights pick them between the darkness, even for just a second. When winds carry them across the lines and into the hair of those driving roof down. When the wolves howl, trees whisper and gravel crunches like bones under worn rubber tyres. Always there, even when it seems like nobody is.

But they're remembered, even faintly. In dreams, in stains and screams. In these songs, these stories. Even when the cars drive back and forth, day and night. When the highway lies empty and dry, so lonely. They'll haunt along the road, fighting with the wolves, reaching for the light, singing together *there's no place like home.*

The gas will take me there and no further. I drink not to water me, I eat not to feed me. The sun finally dips below the mountain. An ancient ache has grown in my bones. The last of my blood seeps into the cotton.

THE HIGHWAY

Everything can change on the road, even when nothing does. Life is always passing in this desert. The highway is as old as the earth it sits on.

Before the sun rises, while a blue moon weighs high, shadows scurry between rocks and cacti, whispering and shivering. Nothing more than something caught in the corner of an eye. They all wait in quiet anticipation.

The car I left by a road stop, keys still swinging in the ignition. A howl from a coyote calls me home. The road is balmy from the day's sun, like someone has warmed my bed.
  I lie down, palms to the earth, eyes to the sky.

So the animals feast, feast on what was left behind—flowers born from blood and tragedy, until they too become lost on the highway.

About the Author:

Georgia grew up in Wollongong and now writes in St Kilda, unable to live anywhere without the ocean nearby.

When not working as a publisher, she is either reading or neglecting a lot of half-baked projects. Her short stories and poems have been featured in magazines and online anthologies including 'Tertangla' and 'Brain Drip'. She is currently working on her debut novel.

She is online at:
I: @georgiamacshanewrites T: @georgiamacshane

CHAOS

B. A. Nielsen

The pain of Crotus' wound eased as he ascended towards the heavens, but his peace was short-lived. The stars were in disarray.

"Ignore them," said Themis. She waved a hand towards two newly placed constellations. "Putting Orion and Scorpio next to each other was Zeus' twisted idea of a joke. He can sort them out."

The scorpion took several opportunities to strike at Orion. When its large tail narrowly missed Crotus, he aimed his bow at the creature's heart.

It froze.

"If you dare move again, beast," Crotus said to Scorpio. "Not even Zeus will protect you from my arrow."

About the Author:

B. A. Nielsen has worked in teaching at universities for many years and published her debut picture book, Otis Paul & Harry the Hairy Echidna, *in 2019. She is also a published Poet with poems included in the Zodiac series by the publisher Deadset Press.*

Having tried her hand at many things, from spinning wool to building an earth house, she now illustrates children's stories, writes in varied genres, and spends time with her beautiful family. You can read her collective poetry on her blog Lifeandbeyondblog@wordpress.com, where she adds some skills as a photographer.

Arrow's Flight

Aveline Pérez de Vera

It is only by drawing the arrow backwards that one can release it forwards.

24th Emmesmonth, 2264
Space Station 3

"Archer, you're up!" said the commander of Echo Squadron.

Archer hawked into the spittoon, grabbed her remote-play goggles—giving them a showy spin around her fingers as she sauntered across the room—and wedged herself into the combat seat. The console was shaped in a large silver arc, with a tall, rotating seat through the middle; it resembled an arrow in a drawn bow aimed up at the ceiling. The seat was still warm from Taylor's body—the lifeless body they'd just carried out. Archer tried not to dwell on that possibility. Warfare had progressed, as it always does, but remote combat didn't mean remote casualties or remote dying. You had to hard-wire into the machines, and once plugged in, death's scythe travelled both ways.

Goggles on, her eyesight adjusted to the vast blackness of space, all the while flexing and rotating her thumbs to limber up. Archer had been picked for this squad on the strength, or rather the length, of those thumbs. Most people's thumbs reached just below their forefinger, but hers were longer, making them the second longest of her fingers. This meant she could operate the flight and firing mechanisms without having to curl her hand. A flat hand could operate for longer, and any army that could pull longer shifts required fewer soldiers. Fewer people on a space station was also a bonus. In a crisis, it meant that all of you might get to eat. So, longer thumbs, longer rations.

They should use that for their recruitment posters, Archer thought wryly.

She glanced to her right and to her left to get the lay of the tri-squad. Smith was gliding his soarer just behind her right flank, and Cooper was bringing hers up to the left, making Archer the lead between them. Basic. Cadet-level basic. Well, it was time to show those dirty Roaches that her squad was more than basic.

A quick low-level scan revealed the enemy amongst the debris of the last battle. They were just hovering below the planet that hung like a large blue ball in the blackness of space, lit from the right by a vast glowing sun. Archer knew that this fiery ball was something she could use to her advantage. A few short commands to her team saw them all manoeuvre their soarers towards the sun.

The plan unfolded with the precision of an atomic clock. The tri-squad held their nerve, making slow steady progress that would lure the Roaches out; their enemy being led to believe the soarers were not aware of them. Archer and her team executed a near-perfect last-minute turn that placed them face to face with their enemy, but with that bright sun now behind them. In the dazzling light, the Roaches couldn't see that Archer's squad had fired up their weapons to the max.

That'll show them something more than basic! The Roaches didn't see what hit them as the bolts of electricity arced across the black sky. Every Roach vessel, now glowing pale blue, drifted away—a dead weight in space.

It was textbook perfect, which is why Archer's death was so unfortunate.

By a stroke of bad luck, one of the ships with typical Roach sloppiness had rotated slightly off formation prior to the strike. The blue bolt from Cooper's gun not only found its mark, but reflected itself back across the void towards Archer's soarer from the unexpected angle of the hit.

In that split-second Archer knew it was over, that she couldn't disconnect herself in time. The flash started at her right temple, burning her ear and jolting down her throat. Trying to squeeze in one last breath, fire filled her lungs. Heat flared down into the pit of her stomach, where her nervous energy for so many years had writhed. Her left leg danced with the overload of borrowed power and her last conscious thought was of all that energy exploding out of her big toe. It took a fraction of a second, but it was long enough to reflect on a lifetime. Indeed, to remember many lifetimes.

Oh, of course! she thought. *I'm on fire—again.*

28th May 1940
L'Epinette, France

Heinz was not yet weary of this war. True, it had only been an official war for around one year, although for him it had been longer. He had joined the infantry as one of the many young and excitable recruits three years ago. The army was a solid career choice, his grandmother said. He looked dashing in the uniform, and he enjoyed the camaraderie. Heinz suspected he was good at being a soldier. Six months after he joined, he was promoted to Assistant Squad Leader. That happened at the time of the successful unification with Austria. He liked Austria, with its pure mountain air. It reminded him of his Alpine home. Not like this low mud-ridden plain they currently occupied.

A low quiet whistle drew his attention. Karl was crouching behind a house wall, rifle pointed down the dark empty street. Only the four remaining riflemen from the squad were on routine night patrol. Routine and boring, as the enemy had been steadily fleeing before the might of the advancing Panzer tanks and German infantry. Those weaklings would soon be cornered with the sea at their backs. The thought warmed Heinz on this fresh night. His squad didn't need to do anything more than maintain their position before the push continued tomorrow. But he was a conscientious leader, and he saw this as an opportunity for them to practise patrol manoeuvres.

At a signal Karl moved forward, and Heinz relocated to the opposite side of the road. They repeated the criss-cross motion a few times more. At the junction ahead they joined Werner and Gunther. All clear. They could now sweep back to the camp by the square, where their squad leader and the three machine gunners were, they hoped, preparing a half-decent meal. Heinz's stomach rumbled at the thought of food. Werner and Karl were holding a low conversation—something about the best way to set a house on fire. He smiled at their dedication. He had a good team.

They rounded the corner into the small square with its stone fountain. The old, worn fountain his squad mocked when they first arrived in the poor French village. This same unappreciated monument now saved their lives as the first bullet ricocheted off the stone, alerting them by a fraction of a second to the danger about to unfold. Instinct took over as they leapt for cover, weapons ready. Gunther and Heinz huddled behind the fountain. Werner and Karl each moved behind a house wall, rifles already firing.

The years of training and combat kicked in. They exchanged volleys, filling the square with noise and smoke. Heinz reloaded. *How was this possible?* There shouldn't be enemy troops nearby.

He estimated the enemy's number based on their firepower, and with a sinking heart realised that his small squad was outnumbered. If they were lucky, they would only be captured and imprisoned. Heinz ground his teeth. Why was there no support from the rest of his squad? No doubt the slackers had been caught unawares and were captured already. Well, that fate was not in his career plan.

Heinz was a good soldier: agile, alert, able both to take risks and to wait patiently, which is why his death during a routine patrol was so unfortunate.

In this modern world where war was ruled by all things metal, a soldier should be safe from assault by wood and feather. Heinz shifted only slightly to one side of the fountain to gain a line of sight to their camp. But he had exposed himself. In a brief break between the rat-a-tat of bullets, the low thrum and whistle of an arrow signalled his fate. He crumpled onto the ground, curled up in pain for what felt like an eternity.

Heinz cradled the feathery shaft with both hands as it protruded from his chest. His uniform that he so dearly loved was changing colour as his blood seeped into the wool, inching its way out into a growing circle. Dazed and confused, he thought he must be hallucinating as he looked up at a British officer holding an ancient longbow in one hand, and a sword in the other.

"Whoa! Mad Jack skewered one, lads! Would you get a load of that?"

More enemy soldiers were coming into Heinz's view. But these soldiers all had rifles, it was only the officer standing above him who clutched a bow. What confidence he must have to face guns with a bow and arrow. At least this defeat was not ignoble. Heinz coughed feebly, his mouth tasting of blood. The world was darkening as his breath slowed. He thought with sadness about his grandmother, his mountain home, his short life. And with his final heartbeat came the memory that drove his final thought—*My luck is ever cursed!*

16th August 1676
Rhode Island

Mitikwab stooped to clear the low tree branch without slowing her run. Her every fibre was focused on flight. She hated retreating, despite its familiarity throughout her life. She had now passed 40 turns of the seasons, and that was long enough to see her land and her people pursued towards oblivion. Mitikwab adjusted her bow lower over her shoulder so as not to snag on the overhanging branches. Her hand found its way to the smooth wood in the bow's centre which always gave her comfort.

She took pride in her bow, her namesake—bow, or arrow, or to stoop, or to serve. The Algonquian language was so fluid. And as one of its warrior chiefs, she could both bow and serve as well as fly like an arrow to clear the path for her people. But for now, she had to run, light as a doe, picking her way across ancient fallen trees on a downhill slope. She could just hear the equally light steps of her men fleeing with her, scattered amongst the forest. Soon they would reach the river.

As Mitikwab ran, her heart ached. What mistakes had she made that led to this retreat? If her husband had not been captured, imprisoned by the invaders, he may have persuaded her to a different course of action. But then, the bond of family was strong, and she would always support the younger brother of her first husband in this necessary war. The thought of one past husband led her to think of the three dead husbands that had followed him. Mitikwab was undecided if fortune had favoured her in love to now be married to husband number five.

She tried not to let her mind wander to memories of the child, though. That grief was still too raw. The great alliance of her current marriage, the joy of a child to unite their two large tribes, and the happiness his little laugh used to bring them had all unravelled around her this last year. But the cause was older. This war was about to continue for a third generation. That's how long the invaders, those who said they were just visiting, had stayed in her land. Her foot slipped, bringing her focus back to the present as she stumbled. But Mitikwab kept her balance and regained the rhythm of the run.

She could smell the river just before she saw it. They appeared as if by magic, stepping silently out of the woods, her men and herself, so few compared to the start of the raiding all those months ago. But they had had their victories, marked with plumes of smoke as each fledgling town burned. How the tide had turned: Mitikwab's people were now attacked as they tried to plant their crops, many slaughtered, others captured and facing a life of slavery. Her thoughts were now dark, in contrast to the water which reflected the light sparkle of late summer. It's cool refreshing feel around her legs held the promise of revival. Once the river was crossed, they could regroup. They would keep on fighting for what was their birthright.

Mitikwab had learned to swim even before her memory of it had formed. It was one of her many strengths, which is why her drowning was so unfortunate.

The strong current unexpectedly pulled her down. She fought it, pushing her bow against the sandy riverbed to lever herself up towards air, towards life. But she was tired, and the current was remorseless, pulling her away from her precious bow, now stuck in the sand, both body and soul drifting further away from it.

As her lungs filled with water, Mitikwab thought of her favourite origin tale: the bow and arrow. The bow had been given by the mother moon, while the arrows were the gift of the father sun. Both were necessary for life, for the bow was a useless tool without its arrows, and the arrows could not fly true without the bow. She had failed. By trying to be both, she had been neither.

As the river took her, she remembered. *Oh, my poor baby!*

28th April 1453
Constantinople

In the still, dark night only one flame shone—from atop the Galata Tower. As the small fleet of ships rowed quietly by Galata's walls, Marco gazed again in wonder at Constantinople, the city across the river that was under siege. He had seen so many unbelievable things. The Ottoman ships being hauled across the hill behind Galata over greased logs was the most amazing thing. But before that, it was the huge chain stretching across the mouth of the river between Constantinople and Galata. The chain that was supposed to stop the Turkish ships entering the Golden Horn.

Well, it did stop them entering by water, but didn't take into account the ingenuity of the Sultan and his men. That was a week ago. A week on tenterhooks with enemy fleets now only a mile from each other on the same stretch of river. Going to war had indeed provided an experience of the world he could never have dreamed about from his small village on the island of Crete.

"Marcello—are you ready?" He bristled at the use of his boyhood name. Just because he was the youngest did not make him less of a man than the others. While he was too young to join the famous archers of Crete when they left home in the pay of the Venetian lords, he had escaped to Venice as soon as he reached manhood. But when he arrived, the Cretan Archers had already left for the impending war in the east. Then the Pope announced an envoy of three ships to support the fight against the infidel, and Marco travelled to Genoa in time to join them.

117

He gripped his bow tighter, remembering the triumphant battle on the Genoese ship as they had fought their way past the massed enemy ships outside the chain to be admitted into the Golden Horn. Marco was not a sailor. He should be with the other archers from home, who were positioned on the far side of the city defending its walls. When he made it through this battle, he would have some tales to share when he joined them. Nobody would doubt he was now a man.

Marco was startled out of his thoughts as the first volley of cannon fire began, so loud after their stealthy progress along the dark river. After that, in the smoke and fiery haze, he could no longer tell what was happening, only that it was happening with great rapidity. He fired off his arrows at the Turkish fleet, or where he thought they might be in the smoke. Sometimes a cry of pain erupted after loosing an arrow and he assumed he'd found an enemy target. Good, because the gunfire, cannons, and arrows were likewise finding flesh in his comrades.

Marco was reaching for the next quiver of arrows when a cannonball shot over the tall merchant ship providing them with cover and plunged through the heart of their galley. As the ship broke apart around him, he grappled to hold onto something, anything to delay the rise of the cold dark water. The last thing he heard were his comrades' cries before the blackness folded around him.

Then he gasped for air, discarding his weapons, armour, and heavy clothes between breaths greedily gulped in. The advantage of growing up on an island like Crete was that its citizens learnt to swim from an early age. Marco managed to keep afloat amongst the flotsam and jetsam and followed the sounds of the other men, both helping and being helped as they swam for the shore.

Blessed relief! He had avoided drowning. Marco said a quick Hail Mary as he crawled up the narrow beach to slump in tired relief with around two score other men, barely half of the ship's crew. As his strength returned, he sat up. Looking out in the dawn light at the wreckage of the Papal fleet, Marco's heart sank. Not just in shame at the lost battle, but because he was looking across the river to the walls of Constantinople.

In the confusion of battle, Marco and the survivors had swum to enemy land. It was such a simple mistake, and one which would lead to his unfortunate death.

The Ottomans wasted no time in rounding them up, and their justice was merciless. Marco was young and not the man of the world he supposed himself to be, for it did not dawn on him at first what the long wooden poles were for. As they were made to lie down in a line along the shore, the piercing screams of his comrades foretold his fate. As his impaled body was raised up in view of the horrified Christian army watching from Constantinople's walls, Marco lived just long enough to think

My God, what have I done to deserve such a fate? And then, in a final flash he remembered.

Winter, 401 BCE
Armenia

Akhilleus and his men took cover behind the trees as the last of the paltry arrows clattered along the path from the hamlet. His blood was still thrumming after the skirmish with the local men half an hour ago. Farmers made poor soldiers, but good sport for a seasoned squad like his Cretan Archers. Akhilleus had volunteered them for this food raid, not just for the black-market potential in an army that was starving, but also because he had grown bored of always running away.

They had been running since Cunaxa. He shuddered at the memory of that last large battle, ransacking the corpses as they lay rotting in the summer sun before their hasty retreat. If you didn't live, then you didn't get paid. A mercenary's life was that simple. And now, months later the snow lay thick around them, their bellies rumbled constantly from hunger, and their feet felt every league walked in retreat from those dusty Mesopotamian plains. Now the battle to win was that of survival; to get home. This army of ten thousand hungry exiles needed to reach the sea.

Akhilleus surveyed the homes, barns, and huts with an expert eye. The women and children were no doubt cowering inside the large house. A lecherous grin crossed his face in anticipation of both sport and food. Why some chose to defend while others gave up and shared their food, wine, and women, he could not say. Over the course of this long march, they had met with both kinds.

"Give us your food," the archer yelled across the winter silence. Did they understand his words? Well, they would understand his actions. He dragged out a young boy captured from the earlier skirmish and marched him closer to the larger hut, his knife hovering under the boy's ear.

"Food! Now, or he dies." Akhilleus had no intention of letting the boy live, not when there was such good sport to be had. The silent youth was on the threshold of manhood, and yet the archer noticed with glee the stain of tears on his dirty cheeks. He hoped he'd picked a mummy's boy, and that mummy was watching now from the hut.

Nearby, animals bleated in fear, and somewhere a woman sobbed. The archer's blood roiled within him. He needed release. Akhilleus gave the signal and one of his men approached, a freshly hewn spike balanced over his shoulder. At least wood was in rich supply at this forlorn outpost. This time the silent boy did cry out, as they impaled his body in clear sight of his home. His cries were matched by wailing from within the hut, echoed by the jeers and curses of the raiding party.

The archer walked slowly around the upright corpse surveying his band's fine work. The kill had raised all his appetites: for food, for death, for a woman. As if rewarded by divine intervention, a flurry of skirts left one of the distant huts. The woman, crouching, fled towards the far woods. Akhilleus gave chase, excited at the prospect of the hunt, the short, ragged bursts of his breath matching his flying feet.

The woman's sobs left a trail as clear as her footsteps in the snow, leading him like an arrow to his quarry. The forest sloped down a gentle hill to where a cold black river eddied and swirled. As the archer closed in, he could see that her crouched posture protected a swaddled baby. He surged forward, the desire for maternal ripe full breasts and soft thighs driving his thoughts of conquest.

With a desperate cry the woman waded into the river, seeking protection in its icy flow. As she pressed deeper into the surging water, she slipped. Her scream turned into a gurgle as she fell and was tugged downstream by the current. Her arms thrust the child above her head, a last despairing attempt to save at least one of them.

Akhilleus watched in stony silence as they both went under, never to resurface. *Well, I'm still hungry, horny, and now even more foot-sore!* As he trudged back up the hill, the archer's mind turned to the hostages still inside the larger hut, sparking a new plan. This one would warm the cockles of the heart.

The bonfire was grand. They shot the fiery arrows in dazzling arcs of light across the darkening sky. The little suns of flame soon ignited the roof of the main hut. The archer heard the panicked screams from within, but there was no escape from this fiery death. His men had barred the door and windows from the outside. Let them all burn from head to toe.

This is too easy. Too basic! The archer's admiration of his work was interrupted by a movement at the corner of his eye. An old woman was creeping towards the burning house, a vain attempt to rescue her family. He howled with laughter, and with one smooth movement raised his bow, arrow nocked, and let loose a spinning shaft. The old woman turned in surprise at the loud laugh, the arrow finding its way deep into her chest. She crumpled onto the ground.

Sauntering over to where she lay, a curled-up ball of pain, the archer sneered down at her frail form.

"Did you think you could outrun my arrows, grandmother?" He smiled. This one seemed to understand him. "You could have avoided all of this. We will still take what you should have given us, and look what you have lost in return!" He spat in her face. The smoke from the fire made his eyes water, but he felt no sympathy.

"You not win," the old woman wheezed in broken Greek, her teeth stained with blood. "But as you curse my family, so I now curse you." She hugged the arrow in her chest, as if it were a friend who would share and lessen her pain. With effort, she released her grip, skin loose with age and thin as paper, as she jabbed an accusatory finger at him.

The archer looked down into dark eyes that glowed with a fury spanning eons. He involuntarily took a step back from the dying crone.

"I call upon the Gods. Witness my bargain. You, archer, shall not die . . ." A wracking cough interrupted her.

"Well, that's a bit of a boon, old hag," sneered Akhilleus, feeling the need to show some bravado before his men. "Giving me eternal life, are you?"

"Shall not die . . . by natural means," she rasped in an effort to finish. "By the father archer Hayk, by the mother goddess Nane, all that you have done will come to pass again. And again. As it was taken, so shall it be repaid. Long may you serve your sentence, archer. Often may you be reborn. Often may you die in pain."

The old woman fell back, dead. On the dark horizon a lightning bolt shot from the purple heavens, shaking the winter ground. The pact was sealed, the fate of the archer had been set, its course as straight as an arrow.

About the Author:

Starting her career as a Linguist, Aveline has never veered far from her love of words. Even as a Training Manager her classes were peppered with names designed to entertain the savvy student (Barb Dwyer, Dusty Rhodes, Brandon Cattle . . .).

An avid traveller to more than 70 countries, she has been spending her travel money during lockdown on collectible books, and her extra time creating more speculative fiction. Aveline's first published story Pride *appeared in the ASF Zodiac Leo anthology. She recently moved from Melbourne to London, where she lives in an open relationship with her books.*

AVELINE PÉREZ DE VERA

LEAD A HORSE TO WATER

Brianna Bullen

She walked into my office. Four legs for days.

God, I loved blondes, especially platinum blondes, and this lady was pure gold. The shirt she wore was cropped to show where her belly met her horse chest, hanging loose off her shoulders. Around this waist lay a belt slung low, weighted with coin purses. Her edges were sharp. Sharp jawline, sharp cheek-bones, sharp walk. Even the fur of her fetlocks was trimmed to a sharp point. The sculptor who had formed her must have been against rounding points. She was a statuesque, a striking sixteen hands high to her human shoulders. Her coat was metallic gold, it made me taste metal on my tongue from biting my lip. Definitely Akhal-Teke royalty.

I took another gulp of water, grateful I'd poured one earlier to stave off my hangover and headache from yesterday's tragic events. Clearly, someone up top was making it up for me, replacing horrors with beauty.

She sauntered over like it wasn't just the ground that was beneath her. Her eyes slid onto me, wavering slightly, before a wide smirk grew across her face, pushing tight skin tauter. "They say you're the best detective around for slimy cases. A lady with a past as patchy as her pelt, but who gets the job done."

"Who says? I'd like to thank the guy for the ringing endorsement."

"Oh, it was ringing," she smirked. "Guy had on his little cowbell and everything."

"Why, lady." I put away the file on the recent cattle-centaur trafficking, knowing I'd be quite thoroughly occupied for the length of this unexpected conversation. Couldn't be thinking of cattle rustlers and shameless hustlers when I had such a fine dame in front of me. "A cattle officer's cowbell is their badge, worn proudly around their neck to show their diligence and service. Mocking a cowbell when it's so earnest as a symbol seems rather cruel."

In a smooth movement—so rehearsed I could barely follow it—she whipped out her nail file from her front pocket, filing down the sharp points into even sharper points. "You mistake me for a kind lady."

I gasped, enjoying myself. "I have done no such thing. Never put a false accusation upon a detective, I can show you the evidence proving you wrong."

She stood comfy in the office, tail flicking as she checked her sharpened nails before she locked our eyes. "And what evidence is that?"

"You walk as if you own the place and the people in it. And that sheen on your hindquarters? You definitely use the Mareine high-end coat powder renowned for being unethically sourced. And you've come to talk to me, a no-good former traffic cop who has gone independent after too many speeding offences."

"I didn't know about the speeding. I always assumed bovine-centaurs couldn't reach a canter. I only knew you were into no-good cases."

"Well, I can reach a full gallop, madame snob, but your intel is correct, I do like no-good, grimy, sleazy cases. What do you have in mind?"

At this she smiled, tilting her head with interest. She stalked over to my desk, putting down a business card over my dossiers of files. From my place at my standing desk, I reached over to pick up the neatly embossed glossy cube of cardboard. The gold foil was the outline of a shield within a square held on a raised dais. In the middle of the shield was a silk-finish 'M'.

My eyes widened, moving between the card and the woman. "You're with Mustang Industry. Trying to find someone who will find him? Forget it. Missing billionaire with his fingers in more pies than a baker? Anyone outside of officials sniffing around that situation is going to wind up a flogged dead horse. Or swimming with the fishes. And I for one am allergic to fish."

"I'm Mustang's secretary," she intercepted before I could get her escorted out of my office. "The board directors and I thought it best to launch our own independent investigation as well as cooperate with the police so we can all figure out what happened and . . . and recover Elone's body if necessary. Please."

She gave me doe eyes, as if those were befitting an equine-centaur at all.

Realizing I would not get rid of her as quickly as I would have liked, I took an old half-stubbed, half fuming cigarette from the mess of my ash tray and put it back between my lips. "Lady, there's nothing appealing about getting involved in Mustang's horseshit. I've been around long enough to recognise a subject too sketchy when I see it. If you're looking for brave and dumb, you chose the wrong PI."

"Would Sunny help if you don't?"

A competitive streak blazoned in me, alongside my need to defend my dippy partner from an obvious snake (as sexy as that snake was) in the grass. She'd only just recovered from a bite on the pastern, I wasn't going to set her up for someone even more venomous.

"Sunny goes where I go. If I say it's too dangerous, she'd trust me that it was too dangerous. No ego to strike out on her own, we're a team." I smiled fondly. "Brains and brawn with occasional brainwaves. Now, what? We all know the man is missing. You've come to nib any suspicion towards you or your associates in the bud? Trying to get us to find you a scape-goat?"

"Not at all," she said smoothly, putting a stack of cash held under a golden horseshoe over the business card. "And no, this isn't a bribe, it's a down payment. Find out what happened, find the body if there is one, and you'll get double that. Capiche?"

I stared at the wad, imagining how many sugar cubes and Spotted Cow beers it would buy me, all while knowing I shouldn't accept it. "Listen, I'll look around. Not going to step on any hooves though, so don't expect any large breakthrough. I'm not risking my neck. Heck, I usually don't accept any payments from suspects. Muddy water, that. And trust me you are not free of suspicion. A company with a deteriorating relationship with their cavalier maverick ruler? Peak motivation right there."

"So you'll do it without payment?" she laughed. "No wonder you're in a crumbling and cramped office behind a laundromat. Good luck on never advancing through society." She reattached the horseshoe onto her belt.

As she sauntered away, tail flicking a fly in annoyance, she glanced over her shoulder. "Please though, detective Deeva. Find Elone Mustang. His vision might just save this fishbowl world."

With his arrogance and exploitation of his fellow centaurs and scarce land? I doubt it, but her concern was the first genuine expression in those eyes and quivering large lips and I wasn't going to challenge her on something she seemed to actually mean. From my experience, there was no arguing with cultists anyway. Lead a horse to Kool-Aid, and watch it drink. I didn't even think our world was a fishbowl. Fishbowls had open tops, and we were more like a glass covered dome floating through space. But instead of arguing like it was a sport, I nodded as I stubbed out my cigarette and put on my trilby.

She then sauntered away, hind-quarters glossy gold, powerful and stocky, her human back swaying above that with feminine grace.

I was getting ready to call Sunny, but we seemed to be sharing a braincell as she entered my office, hindquarters brushing against hindquarters as she and the golden equine-centaur both tried to fit through the narrow door. Sunny did a double-take, eyes wide as they turned to me. "Who the hell was that, Mak?"

I breathed a laugh, giddy from the encounter. "Someone who I'm glad to see the back of, and not just because I like to watch her walk away. We just got ourselves out of a dangerous case, Sunshine."

See, I had no intention of taking her up on her offer. Mustang, the world's richest centaur, had disappeared from his office several weeks ago. The Mustang Institute had tried to keep it quiet, acting like it was just one of the stallion's eccentric travels, but then a dead body had been found, and another, that were alleged to look identical to the maverick creator. Photographs were taken, but the bodies disappeared before anyone could take them in for confirmation or to conduct autopsies. Several later livestreams showed Mustang walking in the background of several locations at simultaneous times. The mysterious situation had felt like an alternate reality game sewn by the Institute in the leadup to the release of their new gaming tech. But Mustang was really missing, according to the secretary. That worried me. The whole situation stunk like cowpat and seemed just as huge and slippery. No amount of doe eyes or simpering stares was going to get me to risk my neck. No intention whatsoever. In fact, I was positive I was going to avoid the situation all together. But when you're sure you've successfully dodged an issue, it will turn up on your doorstep. Or, in this case, an abbey's doorstep.

It was an accidental stumble on our behalf that should have gone to a more competent patrol guard. Only reason Sunny and I were there was Frankel got food poisoning from a batch of hay laced with insecticide, and I owed him a favour. I always paid people back. It's just my bovine nature to be benevolent.

Community patrol was an essential civic duty. It was in our herd nature to protect each other. Sure, we had a police force, but that was mainly just for show. A dressage parade of centaurs in uniform. We all took it very seriously and had a schedule. We had to patrol certain areas at certain times throughout the year, reporting on anything that was suspicious or might jeopardise our precarious world. I'd skipped it once before, fixated on a case. It figures that the time I took up the call, a case would get fixated on me. I wasn't looking for a body, and yet—as Sunny and I trotted leisurely through our route in the religious centre—there it was.

Another body of Elone Mustang.

Elone Mustang must have known something was coming for him. We discovered his body outside of the northern-most abbey, right cheek impaled in the glass roses of the ornament garden, staining it a deep, deep red. So deep it was almost black. The rest of his body had completely crashed through the dome protecting the sculptural gift bestowed to the monastic order back in the era of the thirteenth moon. The ornamental garden was commissioned to replicate our world. A glass dome inside of a glass dome, hurtling through space. Shards scattered around the body like stars on the grass. Elone's body was splayed out on his stomach, limbs positioned at angles that made him look like he was rock climbing horizontally across the ground while his four back legs hung limp. The hooves were coated with red mud from the crypts. That was a curiosity. There were traces of the mud trailing through the grass, imprinted like upside down lipstick kisses.

A lipstick kiss . . .

I rubbed at the fuchsia-pink one Sunny had left just above my collar as I searched for any traces of love making gone wrong and came up shorter than the equine-centaur's Shetland legs. There were no bruises or traces of violence anywhere, save his impaled cheek. No stab wounds. No bullets. No broken limbs. It was like he had just stopped working. Mustang must have hated that. For a centaur who prided himself on working nineteen-hour days, bragging about it in trashy tabloids like *The Daily Stable*, he must have hated his own death. Perhaps a heart attack? But what was he doing at the abbey, especially at that early hour? He didn't strike me as a Sacred Cow follower, rather someone who bought only into the stench of his own shit.

We got to work. We shouldn't have, but I was driven by whatever was in front of me at the time, and Sunny was always going to be mooning over me. While Sunny took photos of the scene, I followed the trail of hoofprints to the door, curious to see none of them actually matched the smaller, cloven prints of the billionaire entrepreneur. All of the marks came from large horses who wore shoes. Mustang was notorious for walking barefoot everywhere, getting daily pedicures, cleans and trims to prevent foundering. He allegedly didn't trust anyone to not nail him with tetanus when shoeing, and with the amount of people he'd pissed off over the years I could see why. Yet, his paid trimmer could have done easily the same, so I believed he did it only for the notoriety. He didn't want to be a man born with a silver spoon in his mouth or silver shoe on his foot. He wanted to be barefoot and honest, in his carefully crafted performance.

The Gothic stone entrance into the abbey was wide and modified to easily allow the arch-bishop's draughthorse hindquarters through alongside another person of moderate hind-girth. There was a scuff across the bottom-side of the wall. But where I expected to see clear, fresh hoofmarks pressed against the dark tiles, there was nothing. There was a scuff on the doorframe. A clipped back hoof on the way out? Walking out and brushing against the door seemed unlikely, given the lack of hoof-prints preceding it. Perhaps he was carried? One extremely large heifer or Clydesdale could do it, but a team of assailants seemed like they'd best be able to immobilise the still powerful kicks of his back legs if they were to drag him out. I needed to explore the abbey, to find out his last movements before his death. To find evidence of anyone else who might have been here at the time.

I'd seen enough barroom brawls to know the best way to take a drunken bull or gelding out was in a security team of three. One for the back legs, one for the front legs, and one to hold the arms down to prevent them punching out somebody's lights as they were thrown out of the building. Two could do in a pinch, if you folded the body forward and grabbed the arms with the front pair of legs. But this was only possible if the person was not resisting. In any case, chucking a centaur out of a building was practically a game to lay them on their sides, fold their upper body in & swing them out once through the doorway. Heck, I'd been tossed out myself. The scramble up was always the worst. Tail between the legs embarrassed, if you weren't too gone with drink to just lay there until morning. The scuff mark suggested he'd gotten a leg free, or that it had been trailing and clipped the door on the way out.

"There's something wrong with the pasture beneath this rich prick's head," Sunny shouted out. "Like someone's dug something up beneath him. And his cheek is—"

"Impaled by glass and a bloody mess? Yeah, I know."

"Nope," she had an annoying habit of popping the 'p,' giving it more pizazz than was warranted, every 'no' a performance to distract from the fact it was a negative. "He's had fillers. And also gotten something dark implanted in them. See? It's like a black tear. Or a smashed insect."

I trotted back over to examine the wound. Sunny pointed to the mark. I leaned over and said "Looks like oil to me. Not quite tar."

"Motor oil maybe?"

"Why would he have motor oil in his cheek? Torture? Experimentation?" I narrowed my eyes, cogs turning with their own motor oil of realization. "Zombies."

Her voice was quiet, as if shocked by my brilliance. "I think the former two are more likely. Or maybe he was concealing something under the skin."

"Most microchips don't have oil leaking everywhere, and business operatives legally cannot be fitted with them. Maybe he was injected with toxic cheek filler?"

"I didn't think it was a microchip," she mumbled, clipped as a well-manicured hoof.

I examined the glass flowers and grass beneath his body, hoping to find a halo of black ink or any trace of a wound beyond his cheek. Other than the superficial graze on his cheek, there really was nothing. Even with the hoofprint, there was no sign of a struggle in the doorway, as the impact hadn't chipped away any of the doorframe whatsoever. No entry or exit wounds—I would roll him over to check his front, but I didn't want my fingerprints all over the body or to disrupt the scene. No obvious cause of death, despite being clearly horse-handled. It was like the body had just shut down between his present position and the doorway.

I glanced to the upper windows in the abbey, trying to not catch on any of the gargoyles and grotesques leering down at me but having the misfortune of making eye-contact with a lion-reptile creature sticking its tongue out at me as it crushed an enemy skull beneath its talons.

Several windows still had stained glass art, opaque and preventing a clear view to the world outside. It showed St Seabiscuit braving the waves to retrieve those otherwise lost in the great floods. The artist had subtly tried to paint over an expression they weren't happy with—one that looked melancholy and a bit bored—and this added to the intensity of the scream. As if keeping a brave neutral face but screaming inside.

From those windows, one could have witnessed the scuffle, whether ward or priest, from this entrance into the vast and layered building. The courtyard was otherwise surrounded by brick walls, although some of the towers could see into it from above, it was long believed that this particular courtyard was only visible to the eye of God and the fellows of that particular wing. God and kin. While the blinds to each of the four rooms were firmly closed shut, there was a definite possibility of a witness.

We shouldn't have trespassed. I hadn't wanted to get involved. But trail was still fresh, so a little breaking and entering meant nothing to me. Cost-benefit analysis, and all that. I was a real mathematician.

Walking through the entryway felt like a heavy weight was placed upon us. Reverence required, even though I was an atheist and solely my own sacred cow. The corridors were made of stone. No comfort of cushioned grass for those who gave themselves up to their God. Every hoofbeat needed to be hard and felt in full, steel against stone. Our shadows followed close as stalker ghosts, lurching like a zoetrope series of images. Electricity was banned here; the hallways were lit by torches, hung up in gilded sconces held on the back of Pegasi sculptures hanging out from the wall.

The lack of activity from those within the Abbey was alarming. What sounded like a shuffle echoed down the stone halls, centred behind one of the wooden doors, but the entire corridor of this wing's stable remained closed. Perhaps they were afraid of whatever they'd heard and were working on unhearing it. Perhaps someone had drugged the sacramental wine trough with tranquilisers. We walked past door after door, turning left and winding deeper into the belly of the beast and still we saw nothing.

"Feels like we're about to be murdered," Sunny whispered, wincing as the sound still echoed down the corridor. The echoing click of our hooves on the stony floor was doing my head in. Here you couldn't even pace alone with your thoughts, always being followed by the echoes of your steps. Hoof beats haunted the hallways as I searched the ground for traces of hoofprints. There was nothing. I'd heard the Abbey was cleaned every night and every morning after breakfast, trying to minimise the scuff marks and to create a cleanly atmosphere. Cover up the dirt of their history. I had hoped that would mean streaks of water and wet hoofprints. But there was nothing. My frustrations were rising, along with bile in my four stomachs. My thoughts buzzed like horseflies, blood pumping hard. Another failure.

And then I saw it. Another foot scuff matching the mud of Mustang's hoof against a doorway.

I smirked, covering up my unease. "I think we might have a possible lead. Whoever is in here might have heard something."

There was a participation ribbon hung up by their door. A simple white rosette with draping ribbons. No colour signalling a higher rank. The person inside was a trainee. He'd be lucky to advance to the purple ribbon of confirmed brotherhood within a year of apprenticeship. This could mean one of two things, which could either help or hinder the case: he wasn't fully indoctrinated within the order and might assist us, or he felt too insecure within his position in the organisation to risk telling us any information. I hoped he was just using the place for board.

"I feel like this place is haunted," Sunny said. "It just has this vibe. It's heavy."

"Nah it's just the lighting and the architecture." She was right that it seemed eerie though, the silence after obvious violence, but she was a horse so easily spooked I wasn't going to add to her fears. The door whined under my fist, the wood old, partially crumbled and flaking. A hand-me-down room.

There was the sound of a startle. Scampering feet as if the shock had made them lose their footing. Then: complete silence. I waited for several seconds. Looked to Sunny. The stillness told me that ignorance was the response that they were going with. The lack of response from anyone in the building made it clear that someone higher up had said something. Or else loyalty ran deeper than justice. Always two faces on the coin of respectability and abhorrence. They would have definitely heard the banging of a hoof striking door.

I was preparing to rear up and kick the door down with my front feet. The door was only made of flimsy wood, and I did like to make an entrance. But then, the door creaked open a peek. I was met with a mule-ish face, mulling on his words. He was a donkey-centaur, his face was young, around twenty. His spectacles were fogged up by morning tea, and when his eyes met mine he reared back and slammed the door shut,

142

presumably to cower in his room, as if trying to hide in the walls while wishing we would go away. A real jumpy kid. We waited him out. There was a muffled swear and then the door opened again. He politely put a hand out for us to shake, face contrite and polite. "My parents raised better than a coward."

He was trembling, so I did my best to be reassuring. "Listen, kid, you won't be charged with accessory to murder or anything just for being in the same place, and we'll protect you if you do say anything as a witness. You don't have to be afraid."

"I hope you're not traumatized," Sunny chimed in, unhelpfully.

Trying to divert attention away from her insensitivity, I glanced around, settling on his bed of hay. "Man, Barley Straw? They're really skimming on the funds, huh."

"We're a bit behind in donations this year," he admitted. "Haven't been able to afford Wheat Straw. It's been painful around here, and not just in sleep."

His whole body, from the tip of his beige head of hair to the sombre line of his back, was slumped like an emotional breakdown.

"You wouldn't happen to know why though, would you?"

"No. I'm a trainee. I keep my head down," he murmured. "Only reason I saw anything last night was the bang against my door."

"Ah," I ran a hand along his bookshelf, seeing dry textbooks concerning Godliness and spiritual life, crafting, centaur biology and CPR (which I assumed was the closest the kid had to Playhorse) and volumes of obscure pre-dome history. Generic lad. "So what did you see?"

"They're my brothers, I can't just dob them in. I'm sure they'll confess eventually," he murmured. "But I don't think anybody was murdered."

I gave him a flat look. "Kid, I'd hate to tell you this, but there is a dead body on your lawn." I peeked over his shoulder and hindquarters. "Ruined some of your pretty plants too."

"He wasn't dead," he crossed his arms over his chest, face the picture of stubborn and youthful rebellion not yet softened by his own mediocrity. "The night was quiet. I just heard a mighty thump against my door. Jolted me right up out of bed when I was finally dozing off. I think they were too busy trying to get his legs under control to see me peeking out. It was like he was glitching. True lightning hooves. Then Father Dought touched something on his neck and he just went completely limp. I'd never seen a dead body before. The way he was just laying there, it scared me. But there were sparks literally coming out of him—I don't think he was ever alive. At least, not as a regular person. Perhaps he truly was magic. The power of electricity defending him. A one-in-a-million show-pony."

"But there were three of them holding him together. Father Tucker Dought who works in the restricted archives was holding his arms, and Stablemaster Ewan Cowder and Bishop Chester his legs. Mustang was completely limp and lifeless in their arms, but then he sparked to life again and just—it was like he was jolted by an electrical current. He kicked out. Caught Chester in the eye, so if you see him around, he's looking long in the face with a shiner. I think they dumped the body in the yard to focus on getting Bishop Chester medical attention. Or perhaps they expected it to be picked up by whoever has been taking in the bodies reported and it would be less of a hassle to just dump it where they could easily get it, while leaving a statement that trespassing is forbidden."

My phone vibrated in my jacket pocket. "One moment to gather yourself, sorry," I said, opening it up.

"Holy shit!1!? This is horse-shit!" the message began, sent from an unknown source. I was reluctant to open the message in case it was spam or a photo of actual faeces taken by someone immature. Perhaps that last exclamation should have been a question mark, and the emailer wanted me to confirm or identify droppings at a crime scene. I didn't want to open it. But I was right to open it. My eyes bulged.

It was from the secretary. She must have been in the company's seedy basement, or else some rare, Elone-private room. Well, private for all Elones, as there was row upon row of vacant eyed, powered-off Elone Mustang clones. Or, if the power cords trailing from their backside-sockets and from their comically well-endowed protrusions was anything to go by, robots.

"Holy shit, Elone Mustang is a robot!" Sunny shouted, looking over my shoulder.

"Elone Mustang made Elone Mustang," I corrected. "Looks like he had a vanity project he kept secret from his company." I was still shocked. Vaguely horrified. Suddenly the public perception that he was 'everywhere' and 'never seemed to sleep' made sense. "A self-made man, huh."

"It's horrifying. An abomination. We were made in the image of God. No false idols. He made his own replica," the trainee said as he looked over my other shoulder.

"Elone Mustang is hardly a god," Sunny said.

I was eager to move on and go to Mustang's Institute to confirm this sight for myself. The hearts in both of my chests were beating harder, pumping my blood through my legs in a way that tingled the hooves and made me want to run towards danger.

"And you can report back that we didn't kill him," the trainee said, crossing his arms. "You can't kill a robot, can you?"

"Depends on how your existential beliefs," I murmured, not wanting to debate anything. I existed. That was my only

146

existential belief. Everything else was confusing. "You got any clue as to why the robot was here? Intel gathering and espionage? Communication with your higher-ups? A performance piece?"

The kid was wide-eyed, as if he'd been handed twelve sugar and caffeine cubes for lunch. "Espionage, maybe? There's a restricted section that only higher-ups have access to. Ancient tomes with ancient knowledge."

"There'd be no risk of real repercussion if it was a robot underling doing the sleuthing and negotiations for him," I inferred. "Any time he wanted info or resources from another organization, he could communicate as himself but not risk his actual life. Or time."

"Seems high risk," Sunny was perplexed. "Why not robots with generic faces and no attachment to his company? No way of tracing it back to him."

"Have you seen any of Mustang's press conferences? The guy wants every credit to go to himself. He wouldn't share anything with anyone, if given half the chance. Also, less risk of the robot investment getting permanently disposed of he'd think it would be too high profile, forgetting how many want him dead. Or maybe it adds to his mystique of an unkillable, undefeatable businessman to his rivals. In any case, we should probably investigate the abbey further. Do you know where the mud of the hoofprint on your door came from? The soil looks almost red, very unique and full of high iron concentration."

The trainee was pensive. Worried, even. "I've seen people return from the crypts with such murk on their hooves. But it is a restricted space. They say it is guarded, so I have never been."

Restricted for trainees, maybe. Restrictions, for people with no attachments, were merely challenges. I left his tiny, cramped study with a swish of my tail and skip of my hooves, Sunny at my flank. Next to her, my shadow on the wall felt huge and strong.

Descending into the abbey was like descending into a nightmare. It was a journey of twisted turns, uniform stone hallways with the same Pegasus candleholders, dim light that got darker as we fell into the bowels of anti-hell. We had yet to hit the red mud. In fact, the floors here were tiled. The terror was in the clean floors. They squealed under my feet, making me super paranoid that I was trailing mud everywhere. Clean floors, and silence. We brushed past a few monks with their bovine smiles of absolute enlightenment, completely silent. Even their footsteps made no sound. I glimpsed a library full of words possibly more ancient than time itself, the shelves glowing gold in lamplight, full of itself in its divinity.

And before we knew it, we were upon the crypts.

There were no doors. It was just a dark, rectangular void, with mud gathering at the entrance. If you looked closely, you could make out the pale grey ramp within the darkness that allowed you to step into the void. However, upon entering, the dark swallowed you and your steps, all that was visible was the next step forward. It was blind faith that you wouldn't encounter any potholes. Sunny bravely set hoof first.

Eventually, we hit mud. The ground tried to hold us, love us, as if reminding us we were part of the earth. It trailed like bubble gum from our hooves as we tore our way through the muck. It took energy to manoeuvre through, the same energy of running through sand or a bog. Hours may have passed, I had no way of gauging the passage of time. It might have been several days, it could have been just ten minutes for us to reach a vault.

Sunny flashed a flashlight at its edges, always ready with a torch. She really was a ray of Sunlight. "Think it opens if you input six-six-six? Nobody would suspect the Devil's number."

I gave it a shot, half-joking, and was surprised when it clicked open. Perhaps they didn't expect anyone to be creeping around the crypts. Perhaps they had a sense of humour. It was a foolish combination.

Maybe Mustang had reset it as a sick joke.

Nothing was found on the body, and yet I was still surprised to find documents inside.

Not just any documents. Schematics. I extracted the mighty tomes, resting them against the top of the vault as I planted my feet in the mud. I blew away the dust, coughing as they painted the inside of my first set of lungs. Sunny and I slowly worked

our way through the documents using the thin light. I was
scanning for something obvious. Something diabolical befitting
a supervillain. I found what I was looking for. My eyes felt
pinprick wide with shock. Jaw dropped. Hands shaky on the
page as I looked over the schematics.

"He couldn't . . ."

But he was Elone Mustang. And for Elone Mustang, he
could do whatever he damn well pleased.

The robot had definitely made its way down here. If it had
recording and transmitting capabilities behind its eyes, and it
hadn't been apprehended in time, we could have been in
trouble.

Mustang Institute announced a public unveiling of their latest
technology three weeks later, on the fall of a public holiday.
With flourish, it was delivered by a centaur in a robe, face
veiled, very obviously a pony.

I was unsurprised to see Elone Mustang up on the erected
stage, acting like the Second Coming with the flourish of a
dressage dancer and gall that only an unscrupulous man such
as himself could possess. His microphone was hovering over
his lip, attached to a wire that disappeared seamlessly into his
hair. Whether this was another bot with a microphone as a
built-in feature remained to be seen, but the messy, overgrown

toe-hooves suggested not. He gesticulated like he was tossing hay with every over-reach.

"News of my death," he smirked, throwing back his veil. "Has been greatly exaggerated."

He winked at his secretary, who glared with unrestrained hostility. Mustang flinched upon not getting his desired claps from her, but turned back to the crowd.

"I have been killed, many times, in pursuit of knowledge for you, the people. I've seen things, recorded things that they don't want getting out."

"What the conmen in government and in the church aren't telling you, is that we've settled around a dying star. 'Surely Mustang', you might say, 'you jest. All stars are dying'. Well, neither the government's files nor correspondence with our leading astronomers suggest we have very long. What they aren't telling you is that they've sacrificed the lives of your children's children's children's grandchildren, and all for the sake of the comfort of the present. What if I tell you we didn't have to die out with the star?" He paused, looking around with giddy glee, high off his own exhaust fumes.

He changed the slide on his slideshow. The screen behind him blew up with an almost identical spaceship schematic that I had seen in the tomes of the Abbey, marked down with materials and features for any potential investors willing to sell centaur-kind out. The design was sleek. Gaudily modern for something that had been hiding out as a forbidden document for centuries "A spaceship, devised by the ancient engineering monks of our world, that can take a select few to colonise other worlds. The physics and mathematics still hold up today. If we put in the resources, we can seed a future for centaur-kind."

A rocket and financial resources in the hands of a madman signalled danger to me. I was but a simple cow, but I wouldn't trust the snake oil sales-Shetland. I was positive his espionage hadn't uncovered anything of the sort, barring the spaceship schematics. But his body had been reported around so many buildings that he could build a story and seed distrust towards the government. Perhaps an uprising.

"And how, you might ask, did I survive? How did I get out of so many precarious situations with my life intact, with all the information? I didn't." On the screen, the image transitioned to photos of Elone Mustang's corpse. Corpses. He had collected several of the beaten robots and piled them together. "I assessed the risks of the information and consequences of spying, and I guessed true. But these were not missions I would entrust to anyone but myself."

That smile. That smug smile. He motioned to the men in Mustang Institute uniforms around him working as security, fading into the background. Only when they were pointed out did the audience realise he was surrounded by clones. Robots. Some were taller. Some had cow backsides. Others had more muscle mass along their chest. But they were clearly made in his image.

"Everything was streamed to me through their gazes. They were my eyes. If anyone needs screenshots for proof, I will provide these. But at the end of the day, what we need, fundamentally, before it's too late, is leadership. A new era in spaceflight. We'll draw lotteries. Look at the qualifications of every citizen and see who is best suited for the task of space exploration, resettlement and multi-planetary living for the majority." He paused to compose himself. "It will be our best and brightest, as well as the most average of Joes. Every ass will have his day. Only if we look elsewhere will our species be able to survive."

He paused again, this time composing his face into a pensive frown. "It will require sacrifice. Especially for those left behind. But selflessness is what the moment needs. "He pleaded with his eyes, his own face projected on the screen behind him, stubby and angular.

"I'm willing to sacrifice everything to see this plan for the future of centaur-kind come to fruition. That's the Mustang promise."

I turned to his secretary who sucked in a breath.

She spoke, every word firm and clipped. "Replicas of himself. He was using them for things like double-booked meetings. Presentations he didn't want to do. Business outings.

And spying on his enemies through recording eyes. Guess he didn't love me enough to tell me he had made robots of himself and would be faking his death and laying low for a bit, huh."

"Maybe he wanted a genuine reaction," I said. "Add to the mystique and surprise of him 'rising from the dead' to give an announcement."

She bristled, the gold of her pelt standing on end like static electricity. "How long do you think this was going on for. Was I ever the real Elone's secretary? The real Elone's lover? How can I trust a damn word that show-pony says?"

"You can't," I said. "He's a snake."

"I smash snakes whenever I rear. I'm not afraid of them." I could tell both her hearts were beating hard, but there was a determined look on her face. "Do you know we got an email today to say every Mustang employee would be severed immediately, replaced by robots? 'The only workers at Mustang Institute will be Mustangs.' The former employees are going to fight for their rights, of course. The man is completely detached from reality."

"The former employees?" I was concerned by her language. The detachment. "You included?"

She shook her head. "I'm through with Mustang. And Mustang is through."

She ran, four legs moving true. The former secretary leapt over the front row of audience members to take the stage beside the Shetland.

"I—" for once, the Shetland was at a loss for words, looking his true size.

She spun around, grabbing him by the throat. Sunny and I moved to intervene, but she was holding tight and we were still several rows back.

"Did you ever love me?"

He choked, spluttered, face red. His front legs were raising off the ground from the force. "You're making a scene—"

"Answer me!"

She lessened the pressure on his throat. The Mustangs working on his security were looking at each other nervously, but had clearly been input with directives not to harm Mustang's former secretary as they stood still. The audience was in shock. They did not know if this was a performance piece.

"The robot who was with you had my neural pathways. He loved you, and I did too—"

"Liar," she said, ramming her nail file into his neck.

We all gasped, but it was not as guttural and blood-filled as the one Elone made. His airways filled up with blood and a large quantity spurted from his neck. He reached out to her, falling to his front knees before his back legs gave out completely and he toppled over onto his side. The colour of the blood—so red, however dark it was congealing—showed this was the real body. Not the tar-blooded replica we found those nights ago.

At the moment her nail-file made impact, I jumped the stage with a shout that was much too late. "Stop."

For a second, it was silent, the golden secretary splattered with red. Sunny was clearly going into shock, terrified that she had allowed the action to happen and disgusted at herself.

The secretary reacted first, slashing me across the sternum in reactive fear and then running fast and weaving through the gaps in the crowd, leaping proud and true over park-goers who had been sprawled out in the sun. All I felt was pain. The red-hot pain that sears across your skin and retinas. Red-out pain. I stumbled, feeling at the wound, staunching the flow. It had not hit any vitals, but it made me falter. Sunny screamed, reaching over to catch me. I tried reassuring her that it was superficial. Nothing to worry about. Even gave a strained smile as I told her I'd be fine.

"Now go catch the golden girl."

She looked after the mad mare, biting her lip and debating the idea of a good ol' fashion horse chase. Faster than any transport, my Sunny. Okay, so maybe it had slashed something more serious than I had thought. Things were getting a bit fuzzy around the edges and I was toppling. I was grateful that

Sunny caught me and helped guide me towards the floor. The grass was so gentle against my cheek. All I wanted to do was nibble on it. I could picture the chase clearly, Sunny galloping faster than any professional athlete, the powerful muscles in her legs propelling her off the ground like a Pegasus before she landed true. Her arms, sharp pistons smoothly cutting through the air. Her hair—god, she'd dyed it a disgusting bottle blonde after my interaction with the murderous secretary—whipping into those fierce eyes.

But she was here. With me.

"She's running towards the ocean," she said, wiping the sweaty hair from my face.

"Maybe I shouldn't have gone so hard on the theatrics," I mumbled.

I could hear the smile in her voice, however strained. "And you call me a show-pony," her hand settled on my ear, rubbing against the felty fur she found. "The seahorse ocean division will get her. Don't worry. They're all around the perimeter."

I laughed wetly, imagining the horse-faced fish jumping out from the ocean to latch onto her ankles, the division trained as a team to wrestle down any larger land centaur. "Bet she won't be expecting that."

Her other hand reached towards the wound, cupped over mine which was staunching the flow until the medic turned up.

It was embarrassing, not the most respectful way I had ended a case. But at least we'd found Elone Mustang's missing body.

About the Author:

Brianna Bullen is a Deakin University PhD creative writing candidate writing about memory in science fiction. She won the 2017 Apollo Bay short story competition and placed second in the 2017 Newcastle Short story competition. Her spec-poetry chapbook Unicorns with Unibrows *is currently out as part of Puncher & Wattmann's Slow Loris series.*

THIS IS THE DAWNING
(PART XII)

Helena McAuley

Twenty-four thousand years ago . . .

It is *not* the Dawning. But it will come soon. We can all feel it.
This Age of Aquarius is coming to an end, and it has been
short. Not quite a full two thousand years. Is humanity ready
for change so soon? Have they surpassed Aquarius' lessons?
Or have they simply tired of them?

Aquarius has called us to this place, once held so dear. It
was the birthplace of a marvel. Now it is a graveyard of sadness.
I pick my way through the rubble of broken towers that litter
once beautiful boulevards. The few slabs of stone that remain
untouched shine like unblemished marble, each a rose growing
in a wasteland. It is silent. All the humans are gone. Either
dead or in refuge in far-off places. There are no birds, no

beasts, none to break the silence. The centre of the city rises before me like a holy mountain, but its edges are lost to the deep, reclaimed by the sea.

Those who lived here called it *Thálassélas*. Those who did not called it blasphemy. Later, they will call this place a folly, they will call it a tragedy. They will call it Atlantis.

We simply called it home.

I crest the peak of the once-bright avenue and descend into the agora where I can see the others waiting for me. The appearance and dress of our incarnations are all those of the Thálassélalonians—flowing, revealing garb. We were all drawn to this place like a beacon. Its beauty and sophistication not seen before in the human world, and we each desired to make it our own. Each chose to be born here, to incarnate here, to live amongst these exceptional humans—now scattered to the sea, now scattered to the wind.

They wait in the resounding silence, sorrowful eyes turned towards me. Each of us bear the grey mark that denotes us as one of the Twelve. The Spirits of the Zodiac, Rulers of the Ages, deigned to incarnate in human form.

My heart is heavy with sorrow for this place, as I know theirs are. Our usually vibrant forms are mellow and subdued with a grief we know not how to express. But none is as weighed down with sorrow and pain as Aquarius—crouched low to the ground in a body allowed to age and wither till I can no longer tell if the incarnation is a man or a woman. Aquarius loved this place more than any of us, and its destruction has taken life from that incarnate form more than the passage of millennia could.

I am greeted. "Φορ Παβιλσαγ, τηε Αρχηερσϵσ Σπιριτ; Ηαλε."

Perhaps I should translate.

"Hale, Spirit of Sagittarius: The Archer and Defender."

It is Capricorn—the Goat-Fish—manifest as a powerful youth, standing so close to Aquarius as to be glued to the withered form; protective, guarded, possessive. Does he think one of us will strike the old one down? Even if it were the Dawning, not here, not in this place, not where Aquarius' heart and soul have been vanquished. None of us would be so cruel.

"I think we can dispense with the pleasantries," I reply. I kneel and embrace Aquarius. "Brother, why have you called us to this place of sorrow?"

Capricorn speaks instead. "Because I asked it."

"Then get on with it, Goat-Fish," Leo growls. "I wish for nothing more than to disincarnate and be alone with my grief."

"But, Leo, so soon before the Dawning?" Cancer asks of him.

"I do not want this Age. And I do not care who does. You can fight amongst yourselves, I haven't the stomach for it."

"There should be no battle," Capricorn states. "I gathered you all here because I have a proposal."

I rise to my feet. "Propose."

"*We* destroyed this place," he begins.

"Lies!" Aries bellows, his eyes flinty with rage. "Each of us loved Thálassélas!"

"Aries," I coo, resting my hand on one massive arm. "Let him speak."

"We destroyed Thálassélas through our ego," Capricorn continues once calm has been restored. "By our bickering and fighting each Dawning. This quest for supremacy must stop. We drag humanity into our grasp, bend them to our will, only for the Dawning to come and shatter that which has been built. We need to decide, here and now, on a better way. We need to decide on one path."

"And I suppose you think that is you," Scorpio spits. "One ruler for all Ages? The King of the Soulless Automatons? Humanity needs *my passion!*"

"It needs *my* joy!" Virgo retorts.

"*I* present balance between the two," Libra sneers.

Bickering explodes between our fellows. Few hold their tongue; Aquarius, too lost in melancholy to enter the discussion. Gemini, watching on as if she may laugh at any moment. And myself. I watch Capricorn as his face contorts at first with astonishment, and then with frustration.

162

THIS IS THE DAWNING (PART XII)

I feel it reach its peak.

"STOP!"

The accompanying, brief, earthquake does not surprise me, but it is enough to silence the others. Their eyes turn to Capricorn with varying shades of shock and fear.

"Stop!" he pleads again. "*This* is exactly what I mean! We are here to *lead* humanity! To *shape* it, not tear it apart! This!" He throws one hand out to encompass all of Thálassélas. "This place was a *paradise!* But it was a prochronism. Humanity was not ready for Thálassélas. And that is *our fault!* We each have something to offer humanity, but we should *work together!* *Build* on each other, one after another, until Thálassélas is no longer a city, but the whole of the Earth!

"Think of it," he continues. "Leo, the lion's strength, tempered with the compassion of Pisces—" he turns from Leo and Pisces towards Aries and Cancer. "—Aries' drive, but with Cancer's equanimity. Scorpio's *passion*, tempered by Libra's justice. My desire for order—" he turns to Virgo and smiles, "—mixed with Virgo's innocent love of the capricious.

"We can rebuild paradise," he says into the enduring silence. "It will just take time."

It is Scorpio who shakes his head. "It won't work."

"It can," Gemini speaks up. "If done properly. And if humanity desires it, also."

"Please, Scorpio," Cancer pleads, slipping her hand into his. "Thálassélas has been taken from us, but if she can be again, please don't let her die a second time."

Scorpio sighs, his face dark with indecision. He pats Cancer's hand. "We should vote. Who here agrees with the goat-fish's scheme?"

"I do."

Their eyes turn to me. "Sagittarius, are you trying to make a joke?" Scorpio growls.

"No," I tell him. "I agree with this plan."

"But you never agree with Capricorn."

"And that hasn't served us very well," I counter. "Make your decisions."

There are murmurs of assent, and some resounding proclamations, but one-by-one, each of the Twelve agree to Capricorn's plan until only one has remained mute.

"Aquarius?" Capricorn asks, his voice soft and tender. "Do you agree?"

There is slow movement in the old bones, like a rumble rising from within to animate the whole. The wizened head rises from the chest, though the grey eyes meet none of ours.

"I will await a new Thálassélas," Aquarius mutters in a voice as dry as sand. "Until that time, let this place return to the sea."

The statement brings the memories of this place to stark focus. The memories of its beauty, and of its destruction. Our grief is renewed in the setting of the sun, casting shadows and silence.

Pisces tentatively breaks that silence. "Who should go first?" he asks.

"That's easy," Gemini replies, a little too flippant for my liking. "Capricorn, of course."

Capricorn's eyes widen with alarm and he begins to splutter. "No! I mean— I can't. It was never my intention to—"

Gemini smiles at him, in that impish way that shows she knows too much. "Did you not think you would have to take *responsibility* for your own design? You are order. Let us establish *order.* We have ignored the procession of the stars. Each build one upon the other, and so should we. By our stars we already have design, but it is inverted. By moving forwards the stars propel humanity backwards, so it is only fitting that we step backwards in order to move forward. Thálassélas was born under Aquarius' reign, let us move back to the time of Aquarius. That, dear Goat-Fish, starts with enforcing structure, it starts with order—it starts with *you.*"

There is hesitance and uncertainty in his eyes, and her words are nonsensical to me, also. But few of us are dim enough to disagree with Gemini when she is speaking from the other realm.

His jaw tightens, drawing lines across his face and brow, but he nods. "Then each of you will support me at the Dawning?"

165

"Not I," Leo states. "I told you it was my intention to disincarnate. This remains my desire. I will not be at the Dawning."

Virgo bows her head, her lips a thin line. "I agree with Leo. Disincarnation seems very palatable at this time."

Surprisingly—shockingly, even—for the second time since time's very beginning, there is unanimous ascent. All wish for disincarnation. All wish to be left alone with their grief. It shocks Capricorn, too.

"I am to be alone, then?" he asks in a small voice, and he seems diminished somehow. "The only one to see out the end of this age of sadness?"

"I will stay," I tell him. His face turns to me and my lips are touched with mirth. "Someone needs to keep you accountable."

There are murmured farewells and some brief embraces. Gemini approaches Capricorn and caresses his arm. "We will return," she tells him. "We just need . . . time." And her lips again hold that self-humoured smile.

Each of them disincarnate, their material forms melting into the aether and releasing their spirits back to the stars.

Capricorn crouches next to Aquarius, as a son may do a father. "What of you? Will you stay with me till the end of this Age?"

166

In the fading light, Aquarius seems even closer to death. As if the body has already passed on, kept animate by only the last threads of resolve.

Aquarius sighs, a deep sigh that rattles his aged chest. "I am sorry, old friend."

Capricorn retreats into himself, his head bowing. "I understand."

"It is for the best," Aquarius assures him.

"Yes."

We watch as the ancient body fades, leaving only a whisper of dust that is caught by the breeze and carried as if to the heavens.

Capricorn stands, and side by side our eyes travel to the sky as the stars make their light first known, rallying against the dying sun. Already Capricorn's shoulders are bowed; weighed with the burden.

I slip my hand into his.

"It's a good plan."

He does not answer immediately. When he does his voice is muted with solemnity. "It will either lead us to salvation, or to ultimate destruction."

"Ignore your foreboding," I council him. "Keep your mind on your goal. Disregard all else."

"Then how shall I know if humanity is ready?"

"Let that be *my* burden."

His grip on my hand tightens as the last of the sun's light slips away, a press of gratitude. "Thank you, Sagittarius."

We stand hand in hand, watching the stars, and waiting for the world to be created anew.

Two nights ago . . .

"Sagittarius."

I stare at Gemini. I have not seen this incarnate form before. She's old. She's ill-kept. She's almost rotting from the inside out. An old woman sitting on the barrier of the bridge and swinging her legs as if she were a child, one shoe teetering laconically from her foot. But her face is lit with youth, and her eyes and lips still hold that same, knowing smile.

"I believe you've been looking for me?" she says.

"Μασηταββα . . ."

She laughs. "Well, if you want to use the old forms, Ηαλε Παβιλσαγ!" She laughs again, this time at a higher pitch. "Oh, this is fun! Yes! Let's speak in Thálassélalonian!"

"No," I cut her off. "I don't think that's necessary."

She shrugs, a precarious thing to do when perched on a balustrade. "Fair enough. But I *do* like this form you've taken." She reaches out to take the cloth of my shirt and run it between her fingers. "*Very* modern. It suits you."

THIS IS THE DAWNING (PART XII)

I shake my head to clear it. She often confuses me. "Gemini," I say to her, "I was not the only one searching. *You* called to *me*, also. Why?"

She shrugs again, and my muscles tense, ready to grab her if she falls. Stupid Gemini, sometimes I wish she'd be serious.

"But I *am* serious," she tells me.

I start. "What—how—"

"Sagittarius, do you still not understand me?" She laughs, then throws her arms wide. "To me the world is wide open! It's a *glorious* feeling! I thought *you*, of all of us, would understand this. You who so long for the return of the spiritual realm. And yet, you can't quite shake your love of the material, can you, my dear?" Again, she takes in my incarnate form, and I am ashamed of the tailored pants and sleeveless silk blouse. She's right, I am vain. I am proud. That is not my only failing; nor is it my only strength.

"And it is your *strength* that is needed now, darling," Gemini continues her not-quite-one-sided conversation.

I shake my head again, frustration rising within me. "Gemini," I caution her, "I called you for council. The Age of Aquarius is approaching—"

With infuriating predictability, she cuts me off. "And humanity is not ready for it."

Finally, she's dropped the foolish act.

"I know, darling. It's a bitter pill to swallow. We've all worked *so hard*. But all is not lost, not yet. The outcome rests on *your* shoulders, my dear. But I need to know that you understand your fears, and your frustrations."

The fears are easy. "Thálassélas tore itself apart because the people were not ready for the New Age." My voice comes out in a terse whisper. "The way humanity is now, if we try to force the Age of Aquarius upon them . . ." I falter, but Gemini gives me an encouraging nod. "They will not survive to the end of it. And then there will be nothing left."

"And your frustrations?" she coos.

"That the rest of the Twelve are too blind or stupid to see the devastation!" The rage explodes from me, ripping from my chest and echoing through the empty streets. Like a bottle under pressure, finding the weakest point, once the stopper had been pulled it is impossible to recap. "Humanity is ignoring the spiritual! Turning away, day by day! They're sending themselves, and this world, into ruin! It is *our* responsibility guide and guard them, but Capricorn is *blindly* obsessed with his stupid *plan!* And everyone else is either so enamoured with it, or so caught up in their own drama, that no one is seeing the *bigger picture!* If humanity dies then the spiritual realm dies with them, and then there is *nothing!* This place—" my arms fling wide to take in the Earth, the moon, the stars "—becomes nothing more than dirt, and rock, and emptiness! And *no one seems to care!*"

In the wake of my anger, my breath is stilted, the human heart hammering inside my chest. I calm myself, and Gemini's lips twitch into a genuine smile.

"Good girl," she praises me. "And now you understand. Don't worry," she continues. "You will have allies. They will not all share your reasons, but they will side with you against Capricorn."

"But not against Aquarius?"

She smiles, that mysterious smile that originates from the other side. "I wouldn't worry about Aquarius."

Despite her dubious advice, I feel stronger, more reassured. I'm already thinking about my allies; Aries, definitely. Pisces, probably not. Cancer, Taurus, and Libra, maybe. At least I will have one firm ally upon which I can build my strategy.

My words escape me with a relieved sigh. "Thank you, Gemini. For siding with me at the Dawning."

She smiles sadly and shakes her head. "Oh, my dear, I won't be siding with you."

"But you said—"

"I have a different role to play," she tells me. "Don't worry, you'll do *fine*. I think you'll soon understand what *I* understand."

"And what is that?"

171

"That existence is nothing but a game; one that is impossible to win, and impossible to lose." Her visage turns bright again. "And that even numbers are an impediment to democracy!"

I sigh and shake my head—the foolish one has returned. "Gemini, you make no sense."

With the warmest of smiles, she reaches out and cups my face. "Yes, I do," she says. "I love you. I love all of you."

It takes me too long to understand. But she knew that even before she spoke, and I guess she was counting on it.

Gemini grins at me and spreads her arms wide. She flings herself from the balustrade and plummets to the street below. With a gasp I grip the railing and lean over the edge. But it is done. She is dead. A broken old woman lying in her own blood and mess, her limbs awry, her face split.

There is nothing I can do. Nothing *to* be done. Even mourning would be a waste of my time. I have more important things to do. I turn away and unmanifest into the night, leaving Gemini how she will remain—grinning up at the sky.

Now . . .

Doug raised his eyes from his feet to the artificial hills and dales of Bicentennial Park. The night-fresh breath of gums, water, and grasses washed over the scattered unit. Leo strode at the fore, while Doug trailing at the rear. They were walking, of course; because of Doug. Because he was still *human.*

The feelings of interconnectedness hadn't lasted long after he'd woken, but that didn't matter, they all knew where they had to go; this patch of green space where his experience had started. Truly started. Not with Capricorn's visit, nor with Pisces' attempts to wake him, but with watching the girl Mia incarnate into Aries. That, Doug felt, was where it had begun. Where he had finally started to understand.

As the small group entered the park and descended the rolling, manufactured hills, Doug's stomach twisted. *This* was the *Dawning.* The final stand. The battle that would decide which of the remaining Twelve would rule the forthcoming Age. People died at the Dawning. *He* may die. Or maybe he would have to kill. Doug wasn't certain which of the two frightened him more.

Maybe he should have called his mum . . .

Their four opponents were waiting for them. Cancer; as sultry and dark beauty as ever. Scorpio; his black-clad and dreadlocked visage all the more terrifying for his recent wounds. Aries, young Mia; haughty and terrible, radiating gleeful anticipation for the battle to come. And Sagittarius; the goddess made flesh.

Doug's chest constricted and he hesitated in his step.

Capricorn was instantly at his side. "What's wrong?"

"Cap." Doug's voice was weaker than even he had expected. "I don't think I can do this."

Capricorn's returning look was tight yet pitying. He grasped Doug's elbow. "It will be okay. I won't let any harm come to you."

Doug swallowed and looked up at the taller man. There was a change to him, one that he had been aware of since he awoke to find Capricorn staring at him. He was calmer, more compassionate, as if the coming of the Dawning had broken the tension that had filled him in the previous days. And he was focused; his bearing and gaze determined. Almost grim.

"I will protect you," Capricorn added into the silence.

Doug believed him. He gave a timid nod and allowed himself to be led.

Sagittarius' voice rang out into the stillness. "Hale, Spirit of Capricorn. Hale to my brothers and sister."

Pisces and Leo did not respond, deferring to Capricorn as de facto leader.

"Hello, Sagittarius," he replied. "We all know why we're here. And we all know what's at stake. There's no need for speeches."

She inclined her head, then turned to her companions. "Vote."

Scorpio spoke first, his voice listing from a slack and drooping face. "I vote for Sagittarius." His ruined left eye was covered by a thick, scarred patch of skin that eradicated the orb, and yet Doug felt it had a gaze of its own that was trained on him.

Leo responded in his booming timbre. "I vote for Aquarius!"

With an enforced decorum that did little to hide the predictability, Aries and Cancer voted for the goddess, while Pisces and Capricorn favoured Aquarius. Of course, the goddess voted for herself. Silence overtook the night, and Doug realised he had become the focus of attention.

"Err . . ." Now what? He wasn't incarnate, would his vote even count? In the chaos and panic of the last two days he'd not stopped to think about this moment. To think about what *he* wanted.

"Douglas," Capricorn prompted.

The words tumbled from his mouth. "I vote for Aquarius."

He was expecting some kind of magic light or energy as the universe accepted the ballot, or some mystic revelation. But there was nothing. Just the dark, and the night, and the silence.

Sagittarius spoke, her jaw clenched, teeth grinding. "The impediment of even numbers."

Doug frowned. What the heck did that mean?

"This needs to be resolved, Sagittarius," Capricorn called to her.

The goddess released a deep sigh of frustration. "I know."

Aries' hand lashed out and a crimson bolt lanced towards Doug. He flinched, arms crossed before him. Capricorn was already moving, but it was Sagittarius' red light that defended him; the flame of her own emanation deflecting Aries' blow.

"Aquarius is *not* to be harmed!" Sagittarius roared at her compatriots, taking to the air.

Aries' head snapped towards her; teeth bared. "Are you *kidding* me?"

"This is *my* command!"

Aries' sneer transformed into a grin as she launched at Capricorn, foregoing emanation in favour of a fist that smashed like a hammer. Leo flew towards Scorpio with a vengeful bellow of rage and a raised fist. Cancer moved to defend Scorpio but was caught by a swath of sea-green light from Pisces that sent her tumbling down the hillside.

Doug recoiled from the carnage and stumbled. But strong hands gripped his chest before he could fall. Capricorn lunged for him, only to be brought short by Aries. Then Doug was in the air, the ground rapidly receding.

Doug screamed and thrashed. Panic overrode him. He couldn't think, he couldn't *breathe!*

"Hush," came a calm voice in his ear. Then the ground was approaching again; fast.

Doug spilled to the ground in a mass of trembling limbs. Blood roared through his ears and he sobbed, once, before he turned.

"Sagittarius?"

The goddess surveyed the battle from the crest of the hill; cold, aloof, beautiful. "This is for your protection," she stated.

Doug tried to swallow, but his dry throat only closed further. "W—why?"

Turquoise eyes of unfathomable beauty turned on him. "You are not incarnate."

Doug stared at her, but her face was unreadable. He turned his eyes to the battle. Scorpio struck Leo with force enough to send the tower of a man to his knees. Pisces and Cancer had taken to the sky, and Pisces barrelled into Cancer and caused the Queen of the Night to fall to the ground. Pisces leapt on her, sea-green fire shining, the placid hippy of her former self unrecognisable.

There was a deep, guttural growl, and Capricorn flung Aries from his shoulders. Face twisted, Capricorn launched volley after volley of burning yellow death at the girl. Aries rolled away from the first, then unmanifest to escape the second. She reappeared mid-air in front of Capricorn, her heel slamming against his mandible and snapping his body sideways.

Doug trembled. Tears burnt behind his eyes. "I didn't want this."

177

Sagittarius' eyes turned on him. He sensed, more than saw, their questioning stare.

Doug shook his head and spoke with more strength. "I never wanted this."

Scorpio ducked an emanation from Leo, side-stepped and came under his guard. With manic glee he thrust upwards into the larger man, and his fist tore through Leo's chest.

Doug shot to his feet. "Leo!"

Leo's face was frozen in shock, a silent scream of pain and horror unable to pass his lips as he was impaled on Scorpio's arm. Scorpio ripped his limb from Leo's body; it was bloodied to the elbow, and in his hand was Leo's heart.

Doug tore at his hair. "*Oh, god!*"

His cry drew a panicked look from Pisces, and the moment's hesitation was all Cancer needed to press both hands to Pisces' chest and send a midnight-blue eruption into her that lifted Pisces through the air and sent her crashing to the ground. Pisces shuddered and coughed. Blood spurted from her mouth.

"*PISCES!*" Doug cried.

His legs collapsed beneath him. His hands clawed at a face contorted by grief. He was going to scream. He was going to vomit. He was going to crumple into sobs and piss and shit and pass out. This wasn't what he wanted. This was *never* what he wanted! The fighting, the bleeding, the dying. This wasn't how it was supposed to *be!*

It was never how it was supposed to be . . .

The air caught in his chest like a punch in the sternum. His lungs burned and his head throbbed as if all his blood was trying to burst from his skull. His heart hammered so hard in his chest he thought it would tear from him. He was dying. He was going to die. And he hadn't even done anything.

And then, he remembered.

Lightning flashed through his body, setting every nerve and cell aflame. Muscles contracted and ligaments stretched, threatening to snap. Every joint locked, straining as if to rip from their sockets. Somehow, he managed to scream, his head snapped back and his neck extended until the veins popped from his skin. He was cradled in agony, held in an embrace of his own destruction. The weight of a thousand lives crashed down upon him; pressing and crushing his mind as *Douglas* was ground into dust.

He *remembered.* Every battle. Every word. Every smile filled with warmth and love. Every sneering fist filled with hate. Eons of loneliness and grief. His sisters. His brothers. Humanity—their children. Joy, and contentment, and isolation, and death.

Thálassélas.

He stood, eyes burning. Panic and fear washed away and replaced with simmering rage.

"*End this*, Sagittarius," he growled.

She watched him for a moment, then her lips twitched into a smile. "Finally."

I do not hear the scream that rips across the battlefield. Nor do I see Douglas's contorted body. But I *feel* his presence; his awakening, his rebirth. We all feel it. Aries and I turn as one, our battle momentarily forgotten.

He stands. A beauteous determination in his bearing. Power, confidence, and certitude in his gaze.

I wish to weep with joy. "Aquarius."

Sagittarius and Aquarius take to the sky, rising until they are twinkling points of red and blue. I make to follow, but Aries lets out a bellow of rage and fires an emanation that I struggle to deflect. The force carries me into a tree that breaks and splits, then erupts into flames.

I hit the ground and Cancer is before me. She grasps my head between her hands and presses at my skull to crush it. I raise my hands to hers, but a blast of sea-green sweeps her from me, scything Cancer in two. Each half is dead before they hit the ground.

THIS IS THE DAWNING (PART XII)

I twist towards Pisces as she struggles to rise. She clutches at her chest, and her bloodied, tear-streaked face is tight with determination through grief. For a moment, my heart aches for compassionate Pisces.

A branch alight with flames falls to my side. I unmanifest away from the blaze, and towards Aquarius. But something is wrong. I cannot retake my physical form. Aries has also unmanifest, and is tangled within me, vying with me and preventing my escape. It is the same tactic I used on Cancer, only hours ago. Duelling whilst unmanifest is not the same as a battle; it is a dance of a million participants. Each cell is converted into *mind*, and it is possible to separate them from the whole. The dance is one of extricating every small, individual mind from those of your partner, without losing control over any piece of yourself.

Does Aries really think she can beat me at this game? She, who has not yet been incarnate for forty-eight hours, against me? I may have forgotten my past, I may not be connected to the greater stream of self, but I know who *I am*.

I pull each filament of my being and slip away from Aries, manifesting so she cannot grasp me again. She is before me in an instant and my emanation explodes from me. She flings herself to the ground before it can hit, and her leg hooks mine a moment after.

My head strikes compacted dirt and turns the world askew. Through the daze everything is in slow motion. Pisces' face is contorted in horror, panicking, Scorpio's arm around her neck. They flicker together but Scorpio yanks her back to the material realm and they resolidify in the same embrace. I can't understand what I'm seeing. Pisces is terrified of Scorpio, yes. He is deranged. But she's better than that. Surely she can best Scorpio, surely her will is strong enough? Maybe.

I raise a hand to help, but my head is slammed back into the dirt and a new wave of vertigo overtakes me. Why can't I beat this? I should be able to withstand more. I *need* to withstand it; need to get to Aquarius.

Aries' fist interlaces with my hair and she wrenches my head from the dirt. Her breath is hot against my neck.

"Watch."

Scorpio tears Pisces' head from her body.

A guttural roar issues forth from my lips. I buck, snaring and thrashing. Aries' supernatural strength keeps me prone. Not Pisces. She has always been the best of us. He killed her, in the most *inhuman* way.

And all I could do was watch.

Scorpio is before me—I didn't notice him unmanifest. His grin is lopsided, the right side of his face still unable to respond. *I* did that to him. I wish I could have done more.

Aries yanks my head higher. Her lustful hiss penetrates my ear.

"Your turn."

Before either of them can move, I am pummelled to the ground by a hurricane pressure. Aries is pressed flat on top of me and Scorpio is blown to the ground. I struggle to turn my head, and in the midst of the gale she lands, glowing with radiant force.

Libra.

She raises her hand and blasts an emanation at Aries, who unmanifests to avoid it. Scorpio is already attacking, but Libra twists and slams her foot into his chest and sends him flying.

My god. She is beautiful.

I regain my feet and stand by her side. Aries and Scorpio regroup. I shift my weight and plant my feet.

"What happened to your plan?"

She sneers, her eyes flinty. "Didn't fricking work, did it?"

I try to hide my grin and fail. It is energising to have her by my side. It feels *right.*

My shoulders tense. Aries crouches low. Scorpio raises his hands.

I glance at Libra. She's grim. She nods.

We strike.

Sagittarius rose higher into the air; and he followed. The corona of red light that surrounded her was a beacon. It matched his own; the corposant blue-flame dimmed to a halo the colour of sky. He barrelled into her and for a moment they both spun and fell. He caught himself at the same time she did, and they hovered, their gazes locked in grim embattlement.

"Call them off, Sagittarius," he growled.

"Why? So you can take your place as Ruler of the next Age?"

"To end the dying!" he screamed. "Incarnation is the only time we can be together. The order was supposed to supplant the battles, but instead of being unified we tear each other apart!"

"And where were *you?*" She shot towards him, teeth bared with accusation and scorn. "Where were you through this last Age? You barely incarnated for your order's crowning glory."

"Because I can't stand it! The hatred, the squabbling, the *killing!* We are brothers and sisters! We're supposed to lead humanity to a greater realm, but you killed Gemini—"

"I *did not* kill Gemini!" Sagittarius snarled. "She took her own life! But Capricorn *murdered* Taurus!"

His blood chilled. "You're lying."

"I am not. Why do you think he never brought you to Taurus on your little tour of appeal? It is because he murdered him. Last night."

"Capricorn— No— He wouldn't—" Uncertainty pulsed within him. Capricorn loved Taurus. He loved them all. And yet . . . He had been different. When he first appeared in Douglas's flat, he was not the Capricorn that Aquarius knew. And he had become stranger still, that morning, when he had assailed Doug with yellow fire. He had been strained. Bent. Ready to snap.

"Capricorn would never . . ." But he was unable to finish.

Sagittarius' gaze was at once piercing and pitying. "Do you even know him, anymore?"

He baulked at that, because it was true.

"Anything he may have done was only to ensure the order."

"Your precious order!" Sagittarius' hands balled into fists of rage and she sailed closer to him. "Is this scheme worth more than the fate of the cosmos? Than the life of humanity?"

"And what life would humanity have under *your* rule?" he shot back. He levelled a finger at her. "I know *you*, Sagittarius. You will turn cities to dust and send advancement back a million years trying to recreate the primordial garden. Humanity should be reaching for the stars. For *us!*"

"Through me they *will* know us! For a thousand generations they have been lost to us, but I will make them see *our* side. You want to stop the destruction? You want to stop the death? You can't, Aquarius!"

He spoke through gritted teeth. "I will merge the material and the spiritual—"

"The realm of the spirit is dead! Not even *you* can balance what isn't there—*I* can bring it back! Your *advancement* will only lead them to destruction! They're not *ready!*"

The wind blew across his hair, scattering it into his eyes. He watched Sagittarius; the rise and fall of her chest, the hands curled into fists, the cast of flint to lips and eye.

"Shouldn't *humanity* decide?"

"They have decided, Aquarius. You're not listening."

He watched her for a moment longer, then closed his eyes, tilting his head and listening to that greater mind that connected them all, the wellspring of consciousness that spawned all things. For the first time in eons he set aside his personal grief and *listened*, filtering out the mundane, the immaterial, until he connected with the heart of humanity. And there was *pain*. Isolation; mistrust; apathy and futility; humanity owned them all. A deep, dark well into which they were not led, but leapt.

And yet . . . Yes. There was also joy, and hope, and longing. Behind the confusion, behind the loneliness, behind the pain, they were all searching for the same thing.

Meaning.

Just as Douglas had always wished for something *more*.

He could give that to them. All those crying minds, all those searching hearts. There could be something more. He could *save* them.

He wanted to save them.

And he saw exactly how.

Libra and I fight as one; always knowing where the other is, always watching each other's back. It is a thing of beauty. It is as it always should have been—she by my side; and I by hers.

I never should have rejected her. I know that now.

Aries and Scorpio approach us from either side. Libra turns and hooks her arm in mine, and I know what she wants. She leaps and we spin, both her feet land in Scorpio's chest. I raise my free hand as I turn and fire an emanation. It hits Aries in the gut and she staggers back. My turn has already taken me too far to follow up, but Libra spins over my shoulder and fires an emanation of her own that tears through Aries' shoulder and sends her to the ground.

I use the force of my turn to smash my fist into Scorpio's jaw. I feel bones in my hand break, but it is no matter. His jaw dislocates and hangs to the side, exaggerating his already slumped face. Libra drops to the ground at the same time I raise my good hand towards Scorpio.

And then I am aware of heat. The grass beneath us has burst into flame and Libra and I are caught in an inferno. It catches my clothes, sucks the breath from the air, and scorches skin. We unmanifest, but damage has already been done. The skin of my legs and one side of my chest is tight and burning, my lungs charred from the inside. Libra releases a hiss of pain, her lips curled back in fury. She's gotten off lighter, but her left leg and arm are raw, and most of her hair has been singed away.

She turns on Aries with a snarl and there is a flash of crimson light. Libra jolts to a halt. She wavers on her feet and I do not make the connection until she is falling. I catch her and she stares up at me—shocked.

I am shocked, too. She's undamaged, except for the flower of blood blossoming at her breast. The emanation was shot with surgical accuracy—right into her heart. I grasp her face and my head shakes. Not now. Not when I have found you again.

Her mouth forms words that take me a moment to understand. *'My kids'.*

And then she is gone.

At first, I feel nothing. And then the ground trembles beneath me, a mere ripple at first, but as muscles tense the shaking becomes more violent. My roar of grief and rage is swallowed by a deep groaning as the earth heaves and splits open. When I look up, Aries and Scorpio are sliding down the newformed precipice of my making even as the quake continues. There is true fear on their faces.

Good.

But not good enough.

THIS IS THE DAWNING (PART XII)

They wanted to watch me suffer. Now I want to *feel* them die.

I manifest and grab Scorpio before he falls into the chasm. Fast as he is, he is not fast enough to escape my rage. The clench of my fist crushes his oesophagus, and my emanation takes care of the rest. Now for Aries.

She has taken to the sky. I am like a comet as I collide with her. She twists and grasps me and we grapple in the air. We are falling. The ground is getting closer. She shoves the palm of her hand against my chest at the same time as I clasp her face.

We both emanate.

Hers hits me like shotgun pellets and my chest is torn apart. That's fine. Mine exploded her head.

I hit the trembling Earth; hard. My spine snaps. My hips shatter. Bones turn to powder and organs rupture. Blood wells in my throat and my lungs. I cannot breathe, all I can do is gurgle and cough.

Wisps of cloud pass the stars and the silence is peaceful. One star moves and becomes brighter, closer. It is blue.

Aquarius.

My quivering lips manage a smile and tears fall onto my cheeks. Aquarius has survived. *Douglas* has survived. The order is complete. The plan is sealed.

Then, it is worth it. It has *all* been worth it.

His feet touched the ruined ground as if alighting from the air was the most natural action in the world. In a glance he took in the devastation and wondered how far it spread.

His eye found Capricorn; broken and bleeding. He, like the ground, was ruined. But already healing.

He knelt beside his friend and lay one hand on his chest. The older man shuddered and spurted blood.

"Aq-uarius."

He smiled. "And Doug, too," he replied. "You were right, it didn't kill me. Just made me . . . Different. More myself."

A breath of air stirred around them, and he looked up to watch the corona of red flame descending.

"Sagi-tarius?" Capricorn spluttered. "Inc-ar*nate*?"

Doug nodded. "It's alright," he said. He squeezed Capricorn's shoulder and stood, turning towards the goddess. "Let's end this," he said to her. "Not with a battle, but with consensus. The way it *should* be. Take the vote."

Sagittarius shot an incredulous glare. "What?"

"Take. The damn. Vote," he hissed back.

She shook her head. "I vote for myself," she said in a cutting tone. "Duh."

Capricorn gurgled, and another wave of blood frothed from his lips. "A-q-*krrk*-quarius!" he spluttered.

190

"I vote for Sagittarius."

Her eyes flashed to his, confused and wary. Capricorn gave a choking growl.

"No," Capricorn wheezed. His face contorted with betrayal and rage. "*No!*"

"I am sorry, old friend." Doug raised his hand. "But it's for the best."

The corposant blue flame flared to life and tore through Capricorn's heart. He sagged into the earth, silent and still.

Guilt and grief pulsed at the edges of Doug's being. He locked them out but could not abate the well of pitying sorrow that opened his chest; making it feel as hollow and shattered as Capricorn's now was.

"That was Capricorn," Sagittarius said. "He always loved you the most."

"He wasn't Capricorn anymore. He needed to rest." Doug looked upon the husk of the once demigod; the broken man. The man Doug had wanted to heal. The man Aquarius betrayed. The chasmal well of longing and loss deepened. If he looked into it, he would shatter.

Doug exhaled and turned away.

Regaining a measure of composure, he smiled at Sagittarius. "What happens now?"

Sagittarius, too, turned from the broken body. "My Age begins. The realm of the spirit must be rekindled. I can do that." She looked out over the ruined park and the city beyond, now her domain. "You were right when you spoke of the primordial garden. The cities *will* turn to dust. Humanity will awaken to the spiritual realm and gladly walk out of them. They will walk in the garden. And then," her voice turned wistful, "I will walk among it, also. Walk amongst *them*."

"The Goddess in the Garden." Doug smiled. "You'll do an excellent job."

Sagittarius turned back to him, her eyes narrow and suspicious. "Why did you help me?"

Doug sighed and looked up towards the fading stars. "I wanted something more," he said. "All my life—all *Doug's* life— I felt like an outsider. I just never seemed to *fit*. At first, I thought there was something wrong with me, then I thought there was something wrong with everybody else. When Capricorn told me I am Aquarius, I thought that was the reason—I *was* separate, something different. But it was none of those things. I'm not the only one. None of humanity *fits*, because we've been separated. We're all pieces to the same jigsaw, but our edges have been smoothed away. You'll bring those edges back so we can connect together again. So we can all fit."

"Interconnectedness with each other and the world."

Doug turned his gaze back to her and smiled. "Individual pieces, forming a bigger picture."

She watched him, scrutinising him with her gaze. "You are different, Aquarius."

"Not different," he countered. "Just more of the same. Besides," his smile turned wry, "I think the grey hair suits me. Makes me look *distinguished*," he said with a theatrical flick of his locks.

Sagittarius groaned and shook her head, hiding the upturned flicker of her own lips.

Doug's smile dimmed to glowing affection and he interlaced his fingers through her hair, drawing her closer and kissing her on the forehead. "Your burden is now lifted, sister. Embrace the world. The material cannot be shut out, nor can it be ignored. But the balance can be carried. Let us try again."

"Thank you," Sagittarius sighed. "For believing in me."

Sagittarius drew her fingers through his and held his hand tight in her own. The sky washed crimson and indigo with the first rays of dawn, and she turned her head to the east. The rosy glow lit her smile. Doug's gaze followed hers, and the grip on his hand tightened.

They stood hand in hand, watching the dawn, and waited for the world to be birthed anew.

About the Author:

Helena McAuley believes that inserting self-depreciating humour into her author bio will endear and humanise her to readers. She's wrong about this, but continues the practice anyway.

When not beset by self-doubt, Helena writes speculative fiction in many flavours, with her favourites being supernatural contemporary fantasy and peppermint-choc-chip.

This is the Dawning has been a serialised debut published throughout Deadset Press' Zodiac series. Helena would like to thank the readers, Deadset Press for taking a chance on her, and especially Austin P. Sheehan (@AustinPSheehan) and Kat Betts (@elementeds) for their tireless efforts in hammering the story into a shape (possibly a rhombicosidodecahedron). Helena also apologises for driving them to drink.

Helena (mostly) twits and (sometimes) instas under @thathmc, is (rarely) facebookified under @thathmc1, and will soon have a website under deconstruction at helenamcauley.com

But what about you, dear reader? Do you think Aquarius made the right choice? Art is interactive, so feel free to discuss on socials using #ThisIsTheDawning

THIS IS THE DAWNING (PART XII)

ABOUT DEADSET PRESS

Deadset Press is an independent publisher of incredible speculative fiction. We provide publishing pathways for emerging writers from Australia and New Zealand, and aspire to shine the light on unique and diverse voices.

You can learn more at:

www.deadsetpress.com

ALSO BY DEADSET PRESS